3

8/2013

The Pony Whisperer

SECRET PONY SOCIETY

JANET RISING

sourcebooks
jabberwocky

Published by Sourcebooks Jabberwocky, an imprint of Sourcebooks, Inc.

P.O. Box 4410, Naperville, Illinois 60567-4410

(630) 961-3900

Fax: (630) 961-2168

www.jabberwockykids.com

First published in Great Britain in 2010 by Hodder Children's Books.

Library of Congress Cataloging-in-Publication data is on file with the publisher.

Source of Production: Versa Press, East Peoria, Illinois, USA

Date of Production: April 2011

Run Number: 14966

Printed and bound in the United States of America.

VP 10 9 8 7 6 5 4 3 2 1

For Kevin

Chapter 1

I HAD HOPED THAT A carefree, Saturday morning ride would push my latest problem to the back of my mind for a while. And in a way, it turned out like that because by the time Drummer and I got back, I had a whole new bunch of things to worry about. "It's so lush here," he wailed, looking around at all the emerald blades waving in the breeze by the side of the newly plowed field, "and it's just going to waste." I pretended I couldn't hear him. If I could keep it up, he might think I'd left Epona behind. He knows that without her I'm just like everybody else; I can't hear an equine word.

"It will be winter soon," he went on, "and there'll be no good grass left. Everyone knows you should let ponies build up fat reserves for the coming lean months. I'm surprised you don't know that. You think you know lots about pony management. Obviously, you don't know as much as you think."

He was trying to rile me, and it was starting to work. My bright bay pony knows exactly which of my buttons to push to get a reaction. I squeezed his sides, and Drum broke into a trot with a theatrical sigh about leaving the grass. I wouldn't mind, but he's already bordering on the tubby side.

Since I'd gone back to school after summer vacation, my riding had been limited to weekends and evenings. With the days getting shorter, evening riding meant everyone jostling for space in the floodlit outdoor school, so that Saturday, it was great to ride in open spaces for a change. We cantered around the field then turned into the woods, Drummer's hoofbeats silent on the moss. Red and golden leaves fluttered unhurriedly to the ground, and there was a damp, autumn smell heralding bleak days to come.

And that's when the first odd thing occurred.

Suddenly, Drummer froze to a halt, shooting me forward. Luckily, as he did so, his head shot up like a giraffe's, keeping me in the saddle. Following the direction of his ears, I could see his gaze fixed on something moving through the trees, and I squinted in the same direction, expecting to see a deer. The woods are riddled with them, and Drummer always overreacts. You'd think they were stegosauruses or something.

It wasn't a deer (or a stegosaurus). It was a pony. An unfamiliar, dark gray—almost black—pony; its black mane and tail laced with white highlights, which glinted silver in shafts of sunlight twinkling through the branches. Catching my breath, I watched as it moved through the trees.

The pony wasn't alone. A girl sat astride the bare, black back. She wore no helmet, and her long, black hair fanned out behind her as her pony cantered and hopped over fallen branches, the pair fused together as though glued. And then I noticed the dog running alongside; a large, leggy hound, like a squire to a knight, keeping his nose level with the girl's toes, matching the pony stride for stride.

I felt the hairs on the back of my neck stand up as the trio disappeared in the gloom. Involuntarily, I shivered. Then I realized that I wasn't the only one holding my breath.

"That's spooky!" exclaimed Drummer, his breath coming out in a *whoosh*, my legs rising against his sides as he exhaled.

"You don't think…" I trailed off, reluctant to put my thoughts into words. The trio had been so strange and had moved so silently. I so didn't want to use the word *ghost*.

The whole area around Laurel Stables, the DIY stable where I keep Drummer, is rich in history and atmosphere. Since Roman times it had been the location of settlements and mansions, taking advantage of the high ground. Drummer's stable yard used to be a farm for a huge country house that no longer exists. It was that history that had given me Epona and changed my life.

I couldn't help thinking that the mysterious rider and her pony and dog certainly looked as though they belonged to a bygone age. I mean, whoever nowadays goes riding without a helmet?

"They wouldn't be the first spirits I've seen around here," mumbled Drummer, snorting. My heart missed a beat, and my thoughts flew back to the séance we'd held at the stables in the summer. Dee had insisted on trying to call up her dead granddad to help us with a team riding competition. The séance had scared us all out of our minds, and I didn't welcome the reminder now, in the gloom of the trees. The woods suddenly seemed very spooky and the very place NOT to be, especially with the wind whispering through the trees.

"What else have you seen?" I asked Drum, winding my fingers through his mane for comfort, half hoping he wouldn't tell me.

"So you *can* hear me?" asked Drum, turning and giving me a look with his big, brown nearside eye. "Pretend you can't hear me when grass is the subject, but you're all ears when there's something *you* want to talk about!"

"Oh, you're impossible!" I said crossly. "You are *not* to eat when we're on a ride, you know that. It's really bad manners, and you'll get green gunk on your bit."

"*Oooooo-eee-oooo,*" said Drum. I couldn't tell whether he was being snarky or whether he was making ghost noises. Either way, it wasn't funny.

At least the strange girl and her pony were a distraction from my own doom and gloom—momentarily, anyway. Things had taken a downward turn at the yard recently, and I didn't want to think about that. The trouble was, the more I tried to block it out of my mind, the more it insisted on creeping back in. Actually, it tended to gallop in rather than creep. It occupied my mind like an invading army, sweeping all good events and thoughts before it and enforcing its dominant, depressing regime at full power.

I made Drummer canter along a path in the woods that we call the Winding Canter (for obvious reasons) and at the end, we burst out of the darkness of the trees and back into the weak autumn sunshine at the top of the hill. Then, without a breather (so Drum couldn't nag me), we walked briskly down the hill to the lane, intending to cross it and continue on the bridle path in a big circle around Clanmore Park, before returning home.

I couldn't stop thinking about the mysterious girl and her pony. That the pony was well bred had been obvious, with its fine legs and neat head. The girl had been slim and had sat easily like an expert rider, her legs relaxed and dangling next to her pony's sides. Wherever had she come from? Laurel Farm wasn't the only stable in the area—there were plenty of stables and farmers who rented fields to the local horsey population. And if she *wasn't* a ghost and if I could get near enough, I might be able to learn more about them—if I could hear what the pony was saying, anyway. At least, I could with Epona in my pocket.

Epona, I had discovered, had been a goddess of horses, worshipped by the ancient Celts and Romans. Ever since I'd stumbled (well, Drummer had done the stumbling, actually) across the tiny stone statue of a woman— Epona—seated sidesaddle on a horse, I'd been able to hear what horses and ponies were saying—for better or worse—whenever I had her with me. I never leave home without her now. To say Epona has changed my life is putting it mildly—I'm known as the Pony Whisperer, for a start, as I can hear and talk to horses and ponies. You'd think that would be fantastic, wouldn't you? But it has its downsides—and was the cause of my latest worry that I had come out to forget.

Halfway down the hill, as we got near to the lane, something happened that did manage to distract me and put my own worries very firmly into perspective. With a droning noise, two huge 4x4 vehicles drove along the road, dangerously straddling both lanes, their lights flashing as they drove past and into the distance. Birds suddenly flew out of the bushes and trees, and a soft hum and clattering from the cars' wake got louder and louder. Familiar sounds of horses' hooves mingled with shouting and revved car engines and, instinctively, Drum and I drew back among the trees, looking down from our natural vantage point toward the approaching commotion. The hoofbeats got louder, the shouts more urgent, more intense, and we waited to see what would come around the bend.

I expected to see horses, but when three came into view, turning the corner abreast and thundering toward us, my feelings of excitement turned to dread.

CHAPTER 2

I WATCHED, HORRIFIED, AS THE horses drew nearer—a piebald, a chestnut, and a tricolored, all in a ragged line. Their brightly colored harness fixed them to three lightweight racing sulkies—little more than two-wheeled frames with a seat for the driver—each occupied by dark-haired teenage boys not much older than me. Stretched across the road directly behind them, another line of 4x4s brought up the rear. The horses had nowhere to go but forward.

The horses were trotting: not the businesslike, working trot Drummer adopts when he's heading for home, but a joint-straining, lung-bursting, whip-enforced, flat-out blur of a trot. I could feel Drummer quivering under me as they bore down toward us.

Racing.

The piebald was clipped out and wore boots on all four legs, the chestnut was thin, its ribs showing through its coat, and when the tricolored horse slipped, the driver thrashed his long, bendy whip on its back and shouted, urging him to make up lost ground. In a desperate attempt to do as it was bid, the tricolored horse broke into a canter, causing the driver to lean back, his whole weight hauling on the reins. I winced as the bit forced the horse's mouth open wide, his chin on his chest as he struggled to return to trot. Going so fast, there was no way he could easily gain control of his legs, and he cantered on, slipping on the asphalt, his driver cursing and pulling even more.

As they drew closer, the smell of burning from the sparks thrown up from their shod hooves on the road mixed with the smell of sweat on their necks and flanks. I could hear their frantic breathing as all the horses desperately drew air into their crimson nostrils, and I felt myself gasping for breath in sympathy. Then in a flash, they swept past with clatters and shouts, and Drum and I watched in sickened amazement as they raced away, the force of the following cars making the last shriveled leaves fall from the shaking branches and drift to the ground around us.

Drummer's ears were anxious, and he snorted in distress.

"Steady, Drummer," I said, stroking his bright bay neck. He was trembling—the race had affected Drummer as much as me. "Come on," I whispered. "Let's go."

We rode to the sandy paths of Clanmore Park where we could breathe pure air and try to get our heart rates back to normal. We were both a bit shaky after what we'd seen— and as we walked along the sand paths, flanked by shrubs and tall grass, I tried to reassure Drum again.

"You all right, babe?" I asked him. "I know it was horrible, what those people were doing to those horses, making them race like that. I'll report them to the horse protection authorities; they'll investigate and make them stop." I knew that when the trembly feeling left me, I'd start to get angry. The trouble was that I didn't know where the horses had come from. I hadn't recognized them—but maybe some-one at the yard would know more than I did. There seemed to be a lot of strange horses around suddenly.

Drummer was all fired up. "Those horses were not only terrified, they were in pain, forced to trot that fast," he said. He shook his head, the shake traveling down his neck, rip-pling through his mane like an ocean wave. It was as though he was trying to shake the image of the race out of his mind.

I knew he was right. The horses were in pain, the strain on their legs must have been horrendous—everyone knows you should trot slowly on the road as it jars a horse's legs—and they were obviously being pushed to their limits. They were scared, too, at being forced to trot so fast. The chest-nut hadn't even looked old enough to do such strenuous work. I felt helpless. I patted Drummer's bay neck again.

"Come on, let's have a canter. You can buck, if you like." Drummer loves putting in the odd buck, just to keep me on my toes. Usually, I'm not impressed, but I was des-perate to pull him out of his unusual gloomy mood and back to his usual sardonic but loveable self.

It was no use; neither of us could get the images we'd seen on the road out of our minds. Retracing our steps back past the road, where all was quiet and normal again, we headed for the yard the long way around. I didn't want to get back until we were both fully settled—even though I didn't hold out much hope for a swift recovery.

So now I had three things on my mind, and it kept jug-gling them around. The sun was shining, and I was with my most fabulous, part Arab, bright bay pony, and I was more miserable than ever. Not only was there the mysterious rider in the woods to investigate, but now I couldn't get the image of the three terrified and straining horses out of my mind. As for my original worry…well, that wasn't going anywhere either.

We were both thoroughly upset, but I wasn't beaten yet. We were going back home via one of Drummer's favorite routes, which I hoped would cheer us both up. Just half a mile from home is a fabulous, big field on a gentle incline, which we all call the Sloping Field. Dotted with trees with a stream in the middle you can jump, it's a great place for a long canter—and if the ponies take off (which they often do if they get wound up), they run out of steam by the time they reach the top, so no one gets carted home.

And that's when I got another shock.

Because the Sloping Field wasn't how I remembered it. The field had visitors—and they weren't the sort of visitors that you invited in for tea.

Dotted around the grass and trees was an assortment of caravans, trucks, vans, 4x4s, sulkies, and horse carts. Among these were horses, all tethered to stakes, and rings were already grazed in the grass. And I could see a piebald, a chestnut, and a tricolored, still sweating from their exertions.

I heard myself gasp as I realized the full implication of what I saw.

The travelers were back.

James was going to freak out.

CHAPTER 3

I DISMOUNTED OUTSIDE DRUMMER'S STABLE, noticing that the stalls on either side of Drum's were empty. Drum's neighbors, Moth and Bambi, were either out in the field or being ridden—and I didn't want to think about their owners riding out together. That was why I'd gone riding in the first place.

"It's quiet around here," mused Drummer.

"Mmmm," I agreed, looking around. Dee Dee's dappled gray mare Dolly was dozing in her stable opposite, her head—covered in a stretchy hood to keep her coat flat—nodding gently over the half door, but the rest of the place was deserted. It only needed some blown tumbleweed to complete the ghost town look. I was desperate to tell someone my news. Where was everyone?

Then Bean answered my prayer by walking out of the tack room accompanied by Mrs. Collins's laid-back brindle greyhound, Squish. (Her name's Charlotte Beanie, but everyone calls her Bean.)

"Oh, you're back. Good," she said vacantly. "What's the more common name for the Asiatic wild horse?"

"Przewalski's horse," I replied, my arms full of Drum's tack. I couldn't imagine why Bean wanted to know, but you never know what wavelength Bean is on half the time. Planet Bean is way out there, nowhere near Earth.

"How do you know that?" asked Bean, frowning.

"Some wildlife program. He discovered them. Actually, I think he was a colonel or a major or something. At least," I added, after thinking about it, "he rediscovered them. I mean, they were always there. But now they're not. They're only in zoos. They're extinct in the wild. But never mind that, you'll never guess what…"

"How do you spell it?"

"What?"

"No, not *what*, I know how to spell *what*," said Bean, sighing. "Prz-what-sit."

"Er, haven't a clue," I said, thoroughly confused. "You'll have to look it up, but I have to tell you about…"

"I can't look it up if I can't spell it, can I?" reasoned Bean.

Having heaved Drummer's saddle onto the rack, I turned and gave Bean a look—wasted, of course. Her long blonde hair spilled over her shoulders, and she was wearing her pale blue sweatshirt inside out. My mom would never let me leave the house like that. And, that reminds me, about my mom…

"You don't look your usual cheery self, Miss Pony Whisperer." Bean grinned, scratching behind Squish's ear. Squish thumped his tail against her legs.

"You'll never guess what I've just seen on the Sloping Field," I said.

"Er…Oh, I know, that TV actor who's just moved into

that big house on the edge of the park. What's his name?" said Bean, closing her eyes in her effort to remember.

I didn't have time for this.

"No, something really awful…" I interrupted.

"Dead body?" offered Bean.

I couldn't begin to guess how her mind worked. "No, shut up and listen—travelers!"

That got her attention. Bean gulped. "Oh. Oh, that's not good. James will go ballistic."

"I know. Where is he?"

"Riding with you-know-who."

I'd guessed as much.

"Well, I'll have to tell him when he gets back," I said. "He'll want to know."

So we waited. I put down Drummer's bed. He was out in the field during the day and stabled at night, now that the nights were getting colder, and I was planning on getting him clipped for the winter. Tiffany already had a trace high—a strip taken off all around the lower half of her neck and body. Bean said that her palomino mare would buck her off if she didn't leave the hair on her back alone. I had that trouble with Drum. There was nothing Drum liked better on a frosty morning than to liven up proceedings with a bucking session. He thinks it's funny. I had decided a blanket clip might at least give me a fighting chance of staying on.

Just as the light was beginning to fade, with swirls of low-lying mist starting to drift across the fields Halloween style, and the birds were winding up their songs before turning in for the night, I heard two sets of hooves clip-clopping along the drive. James and Catriona were back. In the chilled air, I could see James's mare Moth's breath puffing out of her nostrils as she rattled along in her usual hurried fashion, her neck high, her hooves pounding the ground in a permanent hurry.

Grudgingly, I had to admit that the ponies made a good pair—James's bright chestnut with her white face and long white legs blending with Bambi's chestnut and white skewbald coat. Bambi was clipped, too, so her clipped chestnut parts were a lighter brown than the unclipped parts, giving her a three-tone—instead of the usual two-tone—effect. For some reason I can't fathom, Drummer thinks Bambi's just gorgeous. Bambi, on the other hand, always ignores Drum completely—when she's not giving him the evil eye, that is. Flashing me a grin, James pulled up outside Moth's stable, but Cat made a point of ignoring me, as usual. As Cat got busy untacking Bambi, I leaned over Moth's half door and beckoned to James.

"What's the matter?" he said, coming over. "You look serious."

"She is," interrupted Bean, joining me and blocking all daylight from the stable. James flicked on the light, and Moth blinked dramatically as the electric bulb instantly transformed the interior from gloom to dazzling brightness, spotlighting the cobwebs and making the spiders scuttle back into the shadows.

"The travelers are back," I hissed. "Masses of them, camped at the Sloping Field." Travelers are this nomadic group of people who camp in open fields.

James jerked his head toward me, his blond, slightly-too-long hair flicking over his eyes. "Are you sure?" Instinctively, he put a comforting arm over Moth's neck. "Don't worry, Moth," he murmured. "You're safe now. No one's ever going to hurt you again."

"You don't think they'll try to get her back, do you?" asked Bean.

"Of course not, she's mine," replied James earnestly. "Anyway, *they* weren't horrible to Moth, it was those local boys who hung out at the abandoned factory who rode and beat her. All because she was tethered and unable to get away."

James and Cat's brother had caught them. It had happened before I'd moved to the area, but I had heard how they had given the boys concerned a taste of their own medicine before James had untied Moth and taken her away, buying her from the travelers afterward. He'd only recently told everyone else at the yard, and the only thing that had spoiled this heroic story (for me!) was that Cat had shared his secret.

Her story explained why Moth never talked to me, as she trusted only James, and why she was so terribly nervous— even though she was getting better day by day. This could set her back—I could see her ears twitching.

"But I saw them racing three horses along the road,"

I said, the images dancing in my mind as I told them. "Trotting as fast as they could. I mean, *really* forcing them. It was heartbreaking. Drum was badly shaken by seeing them. I'm going to call the authorities and report them."

"It won't do any good," said James, looking serious. "They can't stop them. They did the same thing last time they were here. The animal protection people can't do anything about the tethering either. As long as the ponies have enough food and water, they're not breaking the law."

"What are you all whispering about?" Cat stood by Bambi's door, ruffling her hand through her hair.

It pains me to say it, but Catriona is very pretty. Small, elfin features, short, dark hair, green eyes. And she knows it, too. She wears some peculiar colors together, though, a bit of a jumble, but because she is pretty, she gets away with it. If I wore what she wore, I'd just look as though I'd got dressed in the dark. In a hurry.

"Oh, tell me later, James," she said, giving him a special smile that was more for my benefit than his. She headed for the tack room with Bambi's tack—and even from the back she managed to convey her disdain for me. What a talent!

I looked back at James. He looked troubled. Was that simply because of the travelers? Or could his relationship with Cat be less than perfect?

Because Cat was James's girlfriend. And it was all my fault.

CHAPTER 4

Is THAT YOU, PIA?" Mom shouted as I shut the front door behind me. I don't know who else it could have been, I'm the only other person who lives there with her. There's no room for anyone else in the tiny cottage we moved to when my dad left us to live with his snotty girlfriend, Lyn. I wanted to shout, "*No, it's Santa Claus,*" but instead I meekly replied that yes, it was me.

Mom came bounding down the stairs with her blonde hair tied back and wearing her sweats.

"I'm off," she announced, grabbing her car keys. "There's a salad in the fridge and lots of fruit in the bowl. Try to eat the apples; they're starting to go a bit soft. Don't put those muddy boots on the carpet, OK? See you later, I won't be long."

She kissed me on the cheek, leaving a lip gloss smear, and was out the door.

My mom's latest craze is the gym. Her friend Carol, who's man crazy and always leading her astray, suggested it, and, as my mom is constantly on the lookout for a new man in her life, she agreed that getting toned was a good idea. She's like Dee's show pony, Dolly Daydream. Dee and her mom, Sophie, are constantly trying to hone Dolly's shape—a bit more topline, a bit less crest, strapping her backside to make it just so for the show ring. My mom's doing the same thing—without strapping her backside, obviously. And her goal isn't silver trophies for the mantelpiece—it's a trophy boyfriend.

Well, it's paid off. Her latest boyfriend is Jerry, one of the gym's fitness instructors, and he's younger than my mom. By *four years!* What are the two of them on? Don't go there!

Carol had virtually exploded with overexcitement when she found out. "Oh, Suze," she'd exclaimed, her eyes like saucers. "Sue and Jerry. It's got a ring to it, don't you think?"

"It's a bit early to be talking about rings!" my mom had replied, and they'd both collapsed into peals of laughter like a couple of airheads. Honestly, I know six-year-olds who are more mature. Mom starts off every new relationship full of enthusiasm, yammering on and on about how this one is different—so mature, so full of fun, so considerate, so cultured, so something or the other that makes him perfect, and then, when the novelty wears off, the knives come out. He's boring, he's rude, he's selfish, he picks his nose—there's always something, thank goodness! I mean, if she was to fall in love, who knows what would happen. I don't want to move again, and I definitely don't want some new guy in Mom's life trying to play happy families. I've got a dad, thanks.

The plated salad looked unappetizing. It was the condensation bubbles under the cling wrap—looking like fish eyes staring up at me—that did it. Yuck! Gym membership had included a fitness assessment, training program, and a diet regimen, and unfortunately, because my mom has no self-control, all the delicious stuff we used to eat—Indian takeout, fast food, burgers, pizzas—you know, normal stuff—has been replaced by salad, vegetables, and cuts of chicken and fish so thin you could use them as coffee filters. I spend every spare moment at the stables in the fresh air, riding, mucking out, and grooming Drum. I don't have to watch what I eat!

I stuffed a couple of the apples in my bag—I knew of a certain bay pony that would gobble them up, soft or not—and whipped up some pancakes. At least we still had ingredients for those in the house—although I couldn't guarantee how long that would last.

I couldn't get my mind cleared of all the thoughts rushing around it. As I scraped the eggshells into the trash can, I thought my head was just like it. Me and Mom are always shoving stuff in the trash can and jamming it down until we can't get the bags out without splitting them, putting off the inevitable trip to the garbage can outside until the last possible moment. I didn't think I could force any more thoughts into my brain, it was completely muddled. So I tried to put them into some sort of order.

Which was:

1. The travelers were back. Were they a danger?

When James had filled Catriona in on the traveler news, she had flipped and started raving about them stealing stuff, ranting that we'd have to lock up everything and put a guard on the place. Bean and I had gone a bit pale, but then James pointed out that Mrs. Collins, who runs the yard, actually lives there, and nothing went missing last time the travelers were in the area. And I added that Cat was being prejudiced (which went down beautifully, you can imagine). But there was still a nagging doubt in my mind now Catriona had put it there. But I couldn't think about that because I had number two and the rest of my list to consider.

Which started with:

2. How could we stop the racing?

I had called the authorities, explaining about what I had seen, and they'd promised to look into my complaint, although they'd warned me that there wasn't much they could do.

"Unless they are racing a horse that is sick or lame, our hands are pretty much tied. And it's incredibly difficult to catch them actually racing," the woman on the phone had told me.

And then there was number:

3. What about the strange girl in the woods?

Even though I put two and two together and realized she had to be one of the travelers, I felt strangely drawn to the girl and wanted to find out more about her—talk to her, even. I hadn't mentioned her to the others yet—they'd so flipped out at the travelers' return, they wouldn't be in any state to welcome news that I intended to have a chat with one of them.

And let's not forget number:

4. My original worry: James and Cat were going out together. Why?

When Cat had threatened to get me (and therefore the whole team) disqualified from the Sublime Equine Challenge on the basis of me being able to communicate with the ponies, and therefore, technically, cheating (see, Epona again!), James had persuaded her not to do it by asking her out. Cat had liked James forever (not difficult, he's pretty gorgeous. OK, OK, so you've guessed that Cat's not the only one who has the hots for him!), but until then, he hadn't been interested. So the thoughts I had racing around ever since the two of them started going out were these: Did James ask Cat out just to save the team from disqualification or was that just a convenient excuse? Had he really wanted to ask Cat out anyway? If he had done it just to save the team, then why was he still going out with her?

And then there was the biggest question of all. If James and Catriona got really close, would he tell her about Epona? He's the only other person who knows about her, and we had both sworn to keep her a secret. I lend James the tiny stone effigy from time to time so he can speak to Moth—she refuses to speak to me. I couldn't bear the thought of Cat knowing that my pony-whispering talents were simply down to the luck of having Epona with me. It would make her day—her year, her life!

What if James fell in love with Cat?

What if they went out *forever?*

My imagination ran wild as the questions flew around my brain like popcorn in the microwave.

Ahhhhh! I could never find out the answers without asking James. And that was never going to happen. Can you imagine? I'd die first.

I had to stop thinking about James and Cat. I decided the traveler girl would be my distraction. I was determined to find out more about her. I went to bed worried but feeling better for having a plan. Well, sort of a plan, anyway.

The next day, I saddled Drummer and headed straight to the Sloping Field.

"Why are we skulking around here again?" asked Drummer.

"Shhhh," I hissed, dismounting and parting the branches so I could get a better look at the field's inhabitants.

"What do you mean, *shhhh?* You're the only one who can hear me!" exclaimed Drummer, snatching at the reins and munching on a branch. "Look at these yummy leaves. You should try some!"

"You'd make a terrible spy," I told him, yanking the branch out of his mouth and glaring at him. "James Bond's got nothing to worry about."

"James who?" muttered Drum, yawning.

"I thought you knew everything—he's a famous spy, been in tons of movies."

"And exactly how many ponies have you seen at the movies, wolfing down popcorn and Goobers?" asked Drum, pulling the reins taut as he reached for a tasty tuft of grass.

"You see what I mean? You know about that!" I replied. "Don't be so greedy!"

"Oh, come on, I'll be quiet if I can munch a bit," Drum suggested sneakily.

Sighing, I slackened the reins, and Drum dropped his head like a pony starved as I returned my attention to the travelers' camp.

There were about eight trailers and more trucks and cars, all gleaming. As well as the piebald, chestnut, and tricolored ponies I had seen racing, there was a light bay youngster, a very fat black mare with a mane and tail that looked like they could be contenders for the Guinness record of "longest in the world," two more piebalds, and a gray, all eating circles of grass as far as their tethers would allow. Cropped circles where they had previously grazed dotted the field—they were obviously moved around regularly. I couldn't see any sign of the dark gray pony I'd seen in the woods, or the raven-haired girl—only women and children sitting on their caravan steps or standing talking, and men around the vehicles smoking.

I had come out alone again. Katy and Bean had invited me to ride with them to the old mill, where there were some fabulous hills and dips among the bushes where we could spend a happy half hour riding the ponies up and down the steep slopes, but I was determined to try and see the mystery girl and her pony. I still wasn't one hundred percent sure they were real. Drum had been a bit miffed— he'd wanted to go with Katy and Bean's ponies, Bluey and

Tiffany—but I had made up my mind to find out more, only my plan didn't seem to be working.

"I can't see her," I told Drummer, "or her pony. Only their scruffy, tethered ponies, which all look like they could do with a good groom—including those ones we saw being forced to race. Honestly, it makes my blood boil when I think of those poor ponies being driven along the road. But there's no sign of the girl—maybe she really is a ghost."

Drummer nudged me gently in the back with his muzzle.

"You might want to see this," he said in a rather quiet voice.

"Shhh," I replied, straining to see more.

"No, really, you need to see this," continued Drummer annoyingly.

"See what? Stop it!" I said, turning around to face him. "I don't want to see any more leaves or grass, I have to see whether the girl we saw is with these horrible, cruel travelers...whether she's real..."

When I saw what Drummer was talking about, my mouth stopped making noises.

We weren't alone. Behind us was the girl on her dark gray pony, her dog at her side. The girl wore a sulky expression, and as the dog curled back its lips exposing its teeth, I heard a low, menacing growl.

They were real all right.

CHAPTER 5

"WHAT DO YOU WANT?" snapped the girl, in anything but a friendly tone. She looked down from the sleek back of her pony, her dark features full of contempt. The dog took a step forward, and I felt Drummer move toward it—Drummer wasn't afraid of the dog. He was all for tackling it head on. My crazy, brave Drummer.

"I don't want anything," I said, pulling Drummer back. The last thing I needed was for Drum to get into a fight with the dog.

How could I make the girl believe I wasn't spying on the camp? I so blatantly was, and she was plainly unhappy at my watching her friends and relations. I swallowed, my heart thudding in my chest. This was more than a little tricky.

"I was just out riding," I began breezily. "This is my pony Drummer. Your pony's lovely. What's his name?"

I hoped to strike a more friendly note. Talking about ponies usually did it for me, and I hoped the girl would take the bait and soften.

She didn't.

"Why are you spying on us?" The girl spat back accusingly. She had startling violet-colored eyes, and her straight black hair fell around her face and shoulders. She wore a green sweater, and her feet in sneakers dangled below the frayed edges of her faded jeans. The pony wasn't dark gray—almost black—as it had looked from a distance; its coat was flecked with specks of pure white, as though caught in a snowstorm. Its face and legs were black, and its glossy, silver-laced black mane cascaded over both sides of its neck. The bridle was black, with no noseband, and was the only tack it wore. Chewing nervously on the bit, the pony lifted a front hoof in impatience, its eyes wide, nostrils showing crimson, threatening to whirl away and put distance between itself and us. Its rider, however, held the pony there with effortless skill, her seat and legs preventing it from moving. Steam rose from the pony's flanks, swirling around its rider, making the pair of them even more ghostlike.

But it was the dog that worried me. It looked like a huge, thin, hairy greyhound, with a wheat-colored coat and suspicious, amber eyes. As it took a step toward us, the girl spoke sharply, and I was relieved when it instantly turned, standing again by her dangling foot, its eyes focused intently on us.

"Why are you spying on us?" the girl repeated.

"The game's up!" hissed Drummer, in his very best gangster voice. "You might as well come clean."

This so wasn't the time to be funny.

I thought fast. Whatever lie I told, the girl wasn't going to believe me.

"I was interested in your ponies," I said. "I saw you in

the woods yesterday, and I wondered who you were." The girl's expression didn't alter, so I stumbled on, making things worse.

"I ride around here with my friends. Maybe you'd like to ride out with us?"

"Not so talkative, your rider," I heard Drummer say, doing his best to chum up with the gray.

"Yours doesn't have that problem," the gray replied, her nose twitching. It was a mare.

"What's with your canine pal? He's looking at me like I'm lunch," Drummer said.

"He's all right. Just a bit suspicious of strangers, that's all," the gray assured him. I was pleased to hear that.

Oblivious to the equine conversation running parallel to the human one, the girl spoke again. "Ride out with you? You're either crazy or stupid! Your kind and my kind don't mix," she said. "We never have."

"But we both love horses," I said desperately, not altogether convincingly. "We have that in common."

"I'm Drummer," said Drummer to the gray.

"Falling Snow," offered the gray.

That took all my attention, and my gaze left the girl, settling on her pony in amazement.

"Oh, Falling Snow's a clever name—you have snowflakes on your coat!" I blurted out before I could stop myself.

The girl's eyes widened, and I realized my mistake.

"Oh, nice work!" exclaimed Drummer. "Explain that one, dingbat!"

I couldn't. I felt myself go red. Epona had done it again. But then, I thought ruefully, I was always blaming Epona when I was the idiot. Epona never made me open my mouth and blurt out nonsense; I managed to do that all by myself.

"Who told you my pony's name? Just how long have you been spying on us?" the girl demanded, leaning forward. Falling Snow looked more shocked than her rider.

"It's as though your person can hear me," she said to Drummer.

"Er, well, technically she can. You have no idea how awkward it can be," I heard Drum explain.

I bit my lip. What a total mess.

The girl sat up, her face expressionless again.

"Don't come here again, you don't know what trouble you'll cause," she said sourly, and she turned her pony in one swift movement, cantering off through the trees, the dog bounding after her, its tongue lolling out the side of its mouth like a slice of pink ham.

"Oh, nicely handled!" said Drummer sarcastically.

All I could think about was how well the girl sat on her pony—relaxed and as one with Falling Snow. She had held her on the spot effortlessly, even though the pony had wanted to flee. I wished I could get Drummer to respond to me like that instead of our usual undignified wrestling. I hadn't seen the girl move a muscle, yet her pony pirouetted for her—and she'd sat there, without the security of a saddle, making like a centaur. Not only had I messed up big-time, but I felt a wave of jealousy about the girl's skill with her pony. That she had a way with horses was obvious.

I might be known as the Pony Whisperer, I might be able to talk to Drummer and the other ponies, I might be the person my friends came to in order to find out about their own ponies, but I was a fake. The girl on Falling Snow had a real talent, and it was all her own, not thanks to a little statue as mine was. I felt my heart sink—I'd have done anything to have that girl's natural affinity with ponies. She was more than a pony whisperer, she was a real horsewoman.

CHAPTER 6

I DON'T UNDERSTAND WHY YOU'RE so interested in her," Katy said, peeling off Bluey's purple stable rug. Her blue roan gelding nuzzled her pockets, and Katy produced the treat he knew was there. The stable soon smelled of chewed carrot as Bluey made short, crunchy work of it.

"She's just a traveling girl with a pony. I mean, she's not Ellen Whitaker or anything, is she? And Cat's really got it in for the travelers—she's even more anti than James," continued Katy, flicking a tendril of red hair behind her ear. "She's certain they'll steal all the ponies."

"Well, you can see why she's so worried. After all, Bambi's just the sort of pony travelers take to, what with her being skewbald and all," said Bean.

"You'd better not let her hear you say that," I mumbled. Telling Cat her pony looked like one of the traveler's horses wasn't something I'd volunteer for.

Our meeting room was Bluey's stable. Bean had jammed herself into his old wooden corner trough, sitting with her knees high, her legs dangling, and I sat on an upturned water bucket by the door. Only Katy—wearing shades of purple as usual—was upright, adjusting Bluey's rug and running her fingers through his tail, picking out bits of straw.

It was Saturday morning, and I'd got to the yard early and had already groomed and mucked out Drum. Usually, Bean, Katy, and I meet up and discuss where we can ride or what local events we can take the ponies to. This morning, I had made the mistake of babbling on about the mysterious girl I'd met in the woods. I just couldn't get her out of my mind.

"You should see her ride. And she's just got such a way with horses, a great, natural way," I said, shrugging my shoulders. It sounded lame, now I was saying it out loud. It was difficult to describe the girl's presence to my friends. *They hadn't met her*, I thought. They'd understand if they had.

"Oh, come on, Pia," snorted Bean, swinging her legs. "It isn't like you haven't got a way with horses. I mean, you're the Pony Whisperer, for goodness sake!"

Inwardly, I cringed. Sometimes I forget no one else but James is in on my secret. At least, I hoped that was still the case. My thoughts flew back to my anxieties about James and Catriona.

"Has anyone seen the travelers racing their horses again?" Katy asked, squirting Bluey's tail enthusiastically with conditioner. Bluey tugged at his hay net and chewed thoughtfully, oblivious to what was happening at his rear. (Katy is one of those people grown-ups call capable. She couldn't be more different from Bean, who's all over the place.)

"They were running some horses around in sulkies in

the field yesterday. Dee and I saw them as we rode past," said Bean. "There was a lot of shouting."

"I've never seen this wonder girl you're going on about," said Katy. "Are you sure she exists, Pia, apart from in your head?"

"Well, don't laugh, but that's what I wondered when I first saw them," I said. "I couldn't help thinking about the séance we had in the summer…"

"Oh, don't mention that!" wailed Bean with a shudder. "All those letters, all those horrible words about death being spelled out. I didn't sleep for a week!"

"James pushed the beaker. I kept telling you that!" Katy sighed, the voice of reason.

Suddenly, Bluey's half door flew open and Dee-Dee leaped in, slamming the door shut behind her and making us all jump—including Bluey who stopped chewing for about a millisecond.

"Come in! All welcome!" exclaimed Katy. "It's open house here apparently!" She glared at Bean, who grinned back at her, lifting her legs so that Katy could get to the cupboard her dad had built under the manger. She fished out her grooming kit.

"It's a Twiddles emergency!" cried Dee, looking back out over the door, her brown hair flopping over her eyes.

"In that case, I grant you sanctuary," said Katy, bowing theatrically.

Gingerly, I looked over the door with Dee. Twiddles Scissor-Paws is one of Mrs. Collins's cats and is super unfriendly. He hisses, he scratches, he has everyone on the run—except Mrs. C. With her, he adopts a cuddly kitty cat persona. Everyone else walks in fear of meeting him in the hay barn or seeing him curled up asleep on their pony's rug. Bean's convinced he's the reincarnation of Mrs. Collins's long-dead husband.

We watched the fat tabby strut past with the arrogant air of a cat scared of no one and head toward the tack room.

"Phew, reprieve!" Dee sighed.

"For us, maybe," I said. "What about the mice in the tack room?"

"What are you all doing in here?" asked Dee-Dee.

"Subject? The travelers," explained Bean.

"Oh, nightmare. My mom's changed the padlock combinations on Dolly and Lester's tack boxes. She's convinced we're going to be robbed blind."

Dolly was Dee's show pony, and her mom, Sophie, had a show horse, a liver chestnut called Lester. Sophie is always nagging Dee about her riding, organizing lessons for her in ring craft, and dragging her off to shows. It means Dee tends to whine a bit. Well, quite a lot, actually.

"Why bother changing the combinations?" asked Katy, looking puzzled. "It's not like anyone else knew the old ones."

"You ask her," was Dee's reply, "and let me know how it goes."

"I might. She's always nice to me. I like your mom."

"Yeah, well, it's fine for you, she's not your mom. I get along all right with your mom."

"Yeah, it's funny how that works," mused Bean, picking at the seam in her jodhpurs and making a hole.

"Those travelers have got a really nice blackish pony that would show if it was turned out right," said Dee. "I saw it when we drove past the Sloping Field."

"That's Falling Snow, the girl's pony, the one I was telling you about!" I exclaimed.

"Pia got friendly with one of them," Bean explained.

"What? Are you crazy? Don't tell my mom, whatever you do!" said Dee.

"I am not friends with her—anything but!" I replied. "Although I did offer to be friends—I mean, we're getting ourselves all worked up about the travelers, but has anyone bothered to get to know them? They might be all right."

"They might just be *all right* at swiping things," said Dee. "It's fine for you, but we've got our horse trailer here. They might be all right at making off with that in the middle of the night!"

"You don't know they steal things. We're just making assumptions," I said, imagining the travelers racing down the roads in Sophie's expensive horse trailer. I couldn't see them getting very far—it's the size of a small house. Actually, it is practically a small house—it has a kitchen, beds, even a shower.

"I don't know why you're so keen to stick up for them, Pia," said Bean. "I mean, they might take a liking to Drummer."

"And Dolly's worth thousands!" added Dee.

"Hey, our ponies are totally priceless to us!" Katy interrupted.

"Palominos like Tiffany are highly prized, too. Your traveler friends would take her in a second, Pia!" said Bean, all indignant.

I didn't know how I'd suddenly become ambassador to the travelers—I'd only stuck up for them because of the mystery girl. I couldn't get her out of my mind. I held up my hands.

"OK, OK, keep your shirt on! Jeez, they're not my friends. I was just saying we're being a bit quick to judge them. We don't know they'll take stuff. We're making assumptions."

"Better to be safe than sorry!" muttered Dee darkly.

"I don't like the way they tether their ponies," said Katy, picking out Bluey's hooves. Bluey went into autopilot mode, politely lifting each hoof in turn.

"That's how poor Moth got teased and tormented," Bean reminded us.

Everyone was silent, remembering how Moth had been ill-treated.

"But it wasn't the travelers who did that," I said, thinking I ought to shut up and agree with everyone for my own sake. But my mouth kept droning on, ignoring my brain and better judgment. "It was some boys from the estate!"

"But what about the racing?" said Bean.

I changed sides without a second thought. "That *is* horrible," I agreed. "The poor horses I saw were exhausted and terrified. I don't know why they have to do that."

"Money!" said Bean. "They bet against one another. It's what they do."

"And never mind the poor horses," mused Dee.

"Who's coming riding?" asked Katy, moving the conversation on in her brisk way.

"I am," said Bean, trying to get up out of Bluey's trough. "Oh, I can't, I'm stuck. Help!"

Dee and I grabbed an arm each and pulled until Bean popped out.

"I can't," said Dee. "I have to do some training. Mom's paying 'show pony producer legend' Geoff Chamberlain to come over to give me some last-minute tips. Boorrrring!"

Dee and Dolly had qualified for her show class at the Horse of the Year Show, and Sophie was leaving nothing to chance. She'd dragged Dee off to be fitted for a new jacket, and poor Dolly was rugged up to the nines. The dappled gray looked like the Michelin horse, swaddled from head to hoof in duvet rugs, bandages, and a hood, all to prevent her winter coat from coming through. Drummer had lost his shape to his winter coat already and resembled a fluffy, brown teddy bear, but when the layers were peeled off Dolly, her svelte summer shape showed through her sleek, tricked, summer coat. If the sun was out, she was allowed a layer off. As soon as a cloud loomed, Dee's mom appeared as if by fairy dust (or by broom, according to James) to replace it. Dolly was amazingly good about it all and was excited about the show—much more so than Dee.

"It's the big time, the one everyone wants to qualify for!" I had heard Dolly tell Drummer. "Every show pony dreams of making it to the national level."

Drum had looked at her as though she was nuts. I tried to imagine how he would take to all the pampering and preparation for the national championship. It was as though he could read my mind.

"Don't get any ideas," he had told me. "I don't mind the odd show on a sunny day, but if you ever aspire to all that nonsense poor Dolly has to go through, I'll run off and join the circus."

"You'd soon run back again!" I'd told him. "Two performances a day? You couldn't stand the pace."

"I'm just warning you," he'd said. I hadn't liked to tell him that, handsome though he was, show material he wasn't. Some have it, and some, like my wonderful Drummer, have not. His talents lay elsewhere. I was still trying to discover where, exactly. He's a great all-arounder, but no specialist. But then again, neither am I. My mind drifted back to the mystery traveler girl's talent. One day, with work, maybe I would be as good a rider as her. I hoped so.

"I'll come riding—but let's not go anywhere near the Sloping Field because I don't want to get into any more arguments today," I pleaded.

"Or see any nasty racing!" agreed Bean.

"You've got half of Bluey's breakfast on the back of your jodhpurs," Katy told her.

Bean twisted around and, unable to see the chaff on the seat of her pink-and-now-holey jodhpurs, brushed wildly with her hand. She was wearing a really nice chocolate-brown quilted jacket that I wouldn't have said no to. It looked great with her brown half chaps and made her blonde hair look even paler. Dee had a red waistcoat over her fawn jodhs and her short jodhpur boots, looking the part for her oncoming date with Geoff C. I had on my lime green jodhpurs and orange fleece I'd won in the Sublime Equine Challenge at Brookdale. That had been where James and Catriona had got together. Yuck. Could I just stop thinking about that?

"Where are we going, and who are we going with?" enquired Drummer as I went into his stable with his tack.

"Don't know where, but we're going with Bluey and Tiff," I told him.

"Oh, OK!" he said, pricking his ears and looking pleased.

A car pulled up. Catriona got out and waved good-bye to her dad. I was glad to be going riding. Leanne arrived just after her. Leanne's a bit of a dressage diva, and she and Cat are joined at the hip these days. I'd been the new girl when I discovered Epona, and when the Pony Whisperer thing kicked off Cat had been really huffy. Prior to my arrival, Cat had been the yard guru, the one everyone asked advice from, but when I helped everyone with their pony problems (due only to Epona, of course), Cat got bent out of shape, and as a result, relationships between herself, Bean, Katy, Dee, and James, who had all been friendly with me, had been put under strain. They'd broken down completely when Cat had tried to get us all disqualified at the Sublime Equine Challenge at Brookdale. It made things awkward at the stable— Bean, Katy, and Dee had a history with Cat and were reluctant to be her enemy, but they were also my friends now. Leanne, on the other hand, made no secret of the fact that I meant nothing to her, so she and Cat made a natural alliance.

Drum blew himself out as I buckled the girth. As usual. Then, when I tried to put his bridle on, he pretended his teeth were welded together.

"Open wide," I said, working my thumb into the corner of his mouth, which wasn't easy with the bridle in my right hand, the bit in my left.

Drummer just fixed me with an innocent stare, like he didn't know what I was talking about.

"Wider!" I said firmly.

"Make me," he said. Only it came out "maaaa-meeee," as his mouth was wedged shut.

I sighed. "You won't want feeding ever again, then, if you can't open your mouth," I said sneakily.

The bit slid in. I was fastening the noseband when Bean and Katy rode up outside the door.

"Hurry up, Pia!" shouted Bean. "I haven't ridden Tiff for two days, and she's standing on her head out here!"

I could hear hoofbeats on the concrete. Tiffany was being skittish. She's always seeing shadows in the hedges and is suspicious of practically everything. Bluey, on the other hand, is as solid as a rock. He stood like a statue as Katy tightened her girth from the saddle, dropping her reins and pulling with both hands to force it into another hole around Bluey's ample tummy. He's a little chubby, but he looked less tubby than usual due to his handsome hunter clip—and the feather on his lower legs had been clipped off, leaving them slimmer than usual.

"Is that a new brow band?" I heard Katy ask Bean. Glancing over the door I could see pink and blue crystals twinkling in the autumn sunshine through Tiffany's white forelock. It drew attention away from the fact she wore no noseband due to her phobia about them.

"Wow, Bean, Tiff could be on *Dancing with the Stars*!" I cried.

"Isn't it fabulous?" asked Bean.

I nodded. "Where did you get it?"

"Don't get any ideas!" Drummer warned me gruffly. "I don't do bling."

"Can you get purple ones?" asked Katy, all excited.

"Mmm, I think so, lots of colors."

"Oh, wow, I so want one!" I said, imagining faux emeralds sparkling below Drummer's black-tipped ears.

"It's not happening!" said Drummer. "I don't do tiaras!"

"You don't do anything," I said, leading him out of the stable and over to the mounting block. I passed Moth, and as usual, she shrank back shyly into her stall.

"Oh, that reminds me!" cried Bean, fishing out a hankie

from her pocket as Tiffany shook her head and walked backward toward a tree. "Does anyone know the name of a type of martingale, apart from standing and running?"

"Hurry up, Drummer!" exclaimed Tiffany. "I've a tickle in my toes that won't get itched just standing around here."

"*Just standing?* Are you joking?" I heard Drummer reply.

"Irish," I answered Bean, fastening my riding helmet and pulling on my gloves.

Katy shook her head in disapproval as she watched Tiffany bouncing about. Her pony was still standing as though his feet were nailed to the floor.

"What a total waste of energy!" I heard Drummer sigh in bewilderment.

"What's Irish?" asked Bean, still fishing around in her pocket.

"Ahhh, something's got me!" wailed Tiffany as her tail got caught on the tree.

"The martingale. It's an *Irish* martingale," I replied.

"What does it look like?" asked Bean, as Tiffany catapulted off the tree and started doing half rears, then stopped dead.

"Just a strip of leather with two rings—the reins go through the rings, and then they can't go over the horse's head if the rider comes off. Racehorses wear them," I explained.

"How come you know that?" asked Katy.

"Someone at my old yard had an ex-racehorse, and she always rode him in an Irish martingale and a sheepskin noseband, to make certain everyone knew. Funny thing was, she never went faster than a canter."

"Probably couldn't stop!" suggested Katy. "Ex-racehorses can be total psychos."

"So can some palomino ponies," remarked Drum, and he and Bluey snickered.

"Anyway, Bean," continued Katy. "Why do you want to know about martingales?"

I had pulled down my stirrups and was about to mount Drum when I heard hoofbeats.

"Who's that?" asked Tiffany, curiosity making her motionless for once.

"Who's that?" asked Bean, matching her pony's stare. Katy and I followed her gaze, and I felt my mouth drop open with amazement.

A dark gray pony walked purposefully toward us, its black mane threaded with silver, its dark coat flecked with white. A wheat-colored dog padded silently beside the pony like a faithful servant and sitting easily on the pony's back was the raven-haired girl.

CHAPTER 7

FALLING SNOW CAME TO a halt feet from us all. Everyone was silent in amazement—no one knew what to say. The girl looked at Katy and Bean. When her gaze reached me, she nodded.

"I need to talk to you," she said. "Just you." Her ebony hair, without a riding helmet, was glossy like a raven's wing, her violet eyes like ice. Even though it was a chilly autumn day, she wore the same green sweater and frayed jeans I'd seen her in before. She made such a striking picture, sitting bareback on her strange-colored pony, like a Romany princess. With our waistcoats, hats, gloves, and fluorescent clothing, together with the ponies' saddles and gear, we all seemed suddenly overdressed. It was the oddest thing, like we'd got it totally, stupidly wrong.

Katy looked first at the girl, then at me. I could see her eyebrows rise under her purple silk hat in a questioning manner.

"Do you want us to stay?" she asked me.

I did, but it was clear the girl didn't. I shook my head. "It's all right," I assured her, wondering whether it was.

"Come on, Bean, let's go. Pia can catch up with us later," said Katy, turning Bluey away. Only he didn't want to go. Instead of instantly responding to his beloved Katy's request, the usually compliant Bluey stood gazing at the girl. I glanced at Tiffany. The palomino had abandoned her usual twitchy self to stare at the traveler, too. It was as though she had bewitched them both.

"Come *on*, Bluey!" exclaimed Katy, and Bluey seemed to shake himself, turning as bidden to walk away along the drive toward the bridle path. Bean and Tiffany followed, and I could see Bean looking anxiously over her shoulder at us as Tiffany, back to her old self now the girl's spell had been broken, pranced and danced next to steady Bluey. Drummer gazed after them wistfully, but I could tell he was curious about the mystery girl's appearance. Tiffany, Bluey, and Drummer had all been stunned into silence. That was a first.

I turned to my visitor, my heart pounding. I couldn't think why she wanted to talk to me. Did this mean trouble? I didn't know what to say. Luckily, the girl did.

"I need to talk to you," she repeated, sliding off her pony's back to stand and face me. Her dog moved to her side. "I need..." She hesitated as though reluctant to say her next words. "Your help."

This was unexpected. I blinked in confusion. *What could I possibly do to help her?* I wondered. I was completely thrown. But then Drummer took a step toward her, and she reached out and stroked his face. He stood as though mesmerized, and I heard him sigh. I felt myself draw a breath. This girl really did have a way with horses.

"What do you want?" I said, anxious to break the spell

she seemed to have over my pony; that Drummer felt an affinity with her was obvious.

The girl stopped stroking Drum and returned her attention to me. I wasn't expecting her question.

"How did you know Snow's name?"

How was I going to squirm my way out of this? I thought hard, but no bright idea struck me. The girl spoke again.

"I can remember exactly what you said the last time we met. It was obvious that you weren't talking to me."

Uh-oh, I thought. But what she said next completely surprised me.

"I think you have the power."

I held my breath. She couldn't know. There was no way she could know.

"I think you can communicate with ponies," the girl continued. "You may be *chovexani*, but I'm not afraid of you."

Well, this is a first, I thought. She was ahead of me already. I wondered what *chovexani* was—and whether I was one. I asked her.

"A witch," she said matter-of-factly, as though she knew one or two. I would have laughed, only suddenly, I didn't think it was very funny—especially as she seemed to be the one with powers. I lifted my head and didn't feel afraid to tell her.

"Look," I said, "I know it sounds weird, but I can actually hear what horses and ponies are saying. I'm known as—"

"I need you to talk to Falling Snow," the girl interrupted.

I'd never had such an easy time of explaining away my equine communication skills. Usually I was met with disbelief, with scorn. More often than not, I was accused of lying. This girl not only believed me, she'd believed me even before I'd admitted to it. It was all very strange. And her request sounded like something I could easily do. I'd have a cozy chat with Falling Snow, and the girl would be on her way before anyone saw her. I was getting a bit uneasy about anyone else—Cat or James specifically—seeing us having a little meeting. That would be much harder to explain.

"What do you want me to say?" I asked, looking at Falling Snow. The pony seemed different somehow. When we had seen her before, she had been spirited, full of fire, and keen to be off. Now she stood tired and dejected. She held her head lower, and she didn't fidget. Her eyes were dull. She was a shadow of how she had been before.

"I want you to tell her it wasn't my idea. I need you to explain that my dad was—is—to blame and that I hate him for it. Tell her…tell her I'm sorry…" The girl gulped, suddenly upset and unable to go on. The dog leaned against her.

I was totally confused. What was the girl talking about? I was about to ask her when I heard Snow sigh.

"I know it's not her fault," she said quietly. "I know it is her dad. He said I belonged to Jazz, but he still makes her do what he wants. I don't blame her."

I turned to the girl. "Are you Jazz?" I asked.

She nodded, her eyes wide. "Jasmine," she explained.

"I knew you could hear her. You can hear your own pony, can't you? I thought and thought about what you had said the other day—that you were talking to your pony was the only possible explanation."

She didn't question it. She said it like it was perfectly natural.

"Falling Snow can hear and understand you," I explained. "She says she knows you can't fight your father, that he is to blame."

Jazz ran her hand up and down her pony's mane. "Oh, Snow, I'm so sorry." She brushed the back of her hand across her cheek.

"What did they do to you?" Drummer asked Falling Snow.

"I had to trot, to go faster and faster until I would drop, until I thought I couldn't draw enough breath into my lungs. My back and neck ached, and my legs were on fire. He forced me to go fast, up and down the hill, with my head tied up, to stop me from breaking into a canter. It went on and on, faster and faster, faster still. Today, I can't take a step without every muscle hurting."

"What happened?" I asked. I couldn't help it. I was talking to Falling Snow, but her owner answered me.

"You're *gadjikane*—not one of us," she explained, "but you've helped me. So I'll tell you. Falling Snow's *dya*, her dam, belonged to my mother, and Falling Snow was only a foal when my mother gave her to me. But then my mother died. My dad filled his days with the horse races, and I filled mine with Falling Snow. My dad sold Snow's *dya* on the strength of her speed. He said he could no longer bear to look at her with my mother gone." Jazz took a deep breath and put her hand on her pony's mane.

"In six days, at midday, my dad will race Snow. Snow is fast, like her *dya*. If she wins, she'll be raced again and again and sold on for a high price. I shall lose her. I can see the future as clearly as I see you, if Falling Snow wins the race."

I listened, horrified and unable to put myself in Jazz's place. Her mother dead, her hateful father obsessed with racing the horses—including his daughter's beloved pony. No wonder Jazz went off riding around the countryside. Falling Snow had to lose. Winning the race meant losing her. I could barely believe what I was hearing.

"Snow is too young to race—she's not yet four, but that doesn't matter to my dad. He trains hard, and he trains quickly," continued Jazz. "Yesterday, despite my protests, he harnessed Snow, and he trotted her up and down the field, for a long time. For too long. I shouted, I cried, I threw myself at him. In the end, my dad lost his temper with me. He won't have his *chey*, his daughter, defy him. He put me in my place. Now I know how things stand."

I listened, horrified. I took a step toward her, but the dog growled menacingly, clearly his mistress's guard. It seemed he was the only one allowed to comfort her.

Jazz silenced his growls with a single word, "*Kesali!*" Then she turned back to me. "I need you to tell Snow one more thing," she said.

"What's that?" I asked, wanting to help her.

"Tell Snow to lose. She has to slow down at the end, near our encampment. If she is slow, if she loses, my dad will stop the training and things will return to how they were before. If she wins…" Jazz faltered and stopped. I didn't want to think about what would happen if Falling Snow won.

"I understand," Snow said, so quietly I hardly heard her.

It sounded easy, but I didn't think it would be. Not with Jazz's father getting after Falling Snow like the boys I'd seen racing their poor horses along the lane. It would be impossible for Snow not to try her hardest, being terrorized to race as fast as her legs were capable of taking her—even faster. For a second I imagined how it would feel to be a horse encased in harness, to have a sulky on my tail, the wheels swishing, the driver behind me shouting and beating me along, pushing me until my legs turned to jelly, my breath hammering against my lungs as I struggled to draw in more air, to smell my own sweat and fear as I stumbled onward, desperate to be allowed to stop, unable to protest.

"Snow understands," I told Jazz.

She nodded. "I'm grateful to you," she said curtly. "I shan't trouble you further."

She turned to mount her pony, but then she stopped. Dropping the reins, Jazz turned back to me, looking beyond me toward Moth.

Moth was in her stable, looking out at us, her eyes on either side of her wide, white blaze, nervously staring. Leaving Falling Snow standing with her dog, Jazz walked past me toward the chestnut mare. For a second, I thought she was going say something about her having belonged to the travelers, but she didn't. She walked up to the stable and put her hand on Moth's neck.

I stared in amazement. Moth never let anyone touch her if she could help it—she always backed away, hiding in her stable whenever anyone put out a hand or talked to her, anyone except James.

But not with Jazz. With Jazz, Moth stood steady and strong, her ears forward, her white muzzle pressed into the girl's hand as something special passed between them. I stood openmouthed, witnessing something I didn't understand. Then Jazz walked back, nodded at me, and vaulted onto her pony's dark back. Falling Snow turned without any obvious cues from her rider and carried the girl along the drive away from us—the dog, as ever, padding silently by her side—leaving my mind in turmoil.

What special power did Jazz herself possess? I'd never known anyone apart from James be able to get so close to Moth before. And Drummer loved her, too. He had wanted to be with her.

I was suddenly filled with envy. Even with Epona I hadn't been able to get close to Moth, yet she had wanted to be with Jazz. In that single, shared moment Moth had looked calm. I had never seen her look like that before. Jazz had a true gift that had nothing to do with borrowed magic, the sort I relied on.

Drum was strangely quiet as I mounted, took up my

reins, and headed out to find Katy and Bean. As we cantered along the paths to catch up with our friends, envious thoughts were pushed aside as my mind returned to the reason behind Jazz's visit. Poor Falling Snow was a slave to Jazz's father, and Jazz was powerless to intervene. The image of Snow, exhausted, betrayed, and dejected, so different from the proud, spirited pony I had first seen, haunted me.

I knew one thing: I had to see for myself how Falling Snow fared in the race. I had to see with my own eyes whether she had the strength to resist the power and will of Jazz's dad, or whether she would be forced against her own will to go faster than she'd ever gone before and seal her own fate.

Whatever that fate would be.

CHAPTER 8

I DIDN'T WANT TO TAKE Drummer; the sight of the horses being hurried along before had so upset him, and I didn't want him to go through that again. I was really nervous about going on my own—what with all my mom's dire warnings: the ones about not going riding alone (I did do that, but I sort of banked on Drum taking care of me), and riding my bike home before it got dark, and never walking through the woods on my own.

So I had agonized over whether to ask Bean to go with me, but in the end, my courage failed me as I remembered how she and Katy had refused to give Jazz a chance. They had both been a bit uneasy about Jazz coming to the yard, but I'd assured them it was only once and they were satisfied I hadn't invited her. With all the anti-Jazz feeling around, I couldn't risk the others knowing I was going to watch the race. My courage failed me twice because if I had been brave enough, I would have stood up for Jazz and Falling Snow. I had so many mixed feelings, I had to go alone and hope I could get it all sorted out in my own mind.

I knew I needed to be at the finish of the race, and it wasn't very far to walk. As I set off that Saturday, making sure no one saw me, my brain returned to the big questions facing Falling Snow. Would the mare be able to ignore the whip and the shouting and lose the race? I kicked fallen chestnuts and leaves as I hurried along the bridle path, keeping a lookout for approaching ponies and their curious and disapproving riders.

The woods seemed much bigger on foot than when I rode through them on Drum. I was beginning to puff a bit and starting to feel a tiny bit of sympathy for my pony. I made up my mind I wouldn't tell him that. Can you imagine? He'd never let it go, would he?

At last I got near to the place where the race was due to end—but I didn't want to get too close, for obvious reasons. Sure enough, there was a small gathering of travelers at the end of the lane, so I retreated along a footpath, which led up a hill along a hedge on the edge of a farmer's field, to trees forming a small copse at the top. From this vantage point, I could look down at the lane and the waiting group.

Travelers had blocked the lane with their vehicles, forming a barrier so that no one could enter. They stood about smoking, talking, glancing along the lane, anxious to catch a glimpse of the approaching horses. Money was still changing hands—I saw a wad of bills passed from one man to the other—and dogs sat next to their masters or scratched behind their ears with a hind foot. There seemed to be a lot of that going on.

I couldn't tell whether my heart was thudding because I'd climbed the hill or because I was so nervous. I hoped I wouldn't have to wait too long. The sky was gray and angry, with dark rain clouds sweeping in toward me, and the wind howled up the hill. I dug my hands into my jacket pockets to keep them warm. Curling my fingers around Epona who was buried deep in one of them, I felt my heart sink. Did I really want to hear what the racing horses had to say?

"You had to see," said a voice, making me jump like a startled rabbit. Whirling around, I saw Jazz and her dog walking out of the trees.

I gave her a sort of half grin. The wheat-colored hound stayed close to Jazz, leaning against her leg, his eyes trained on me. I felt strangely vulnerable without Drummer. What if the dog went for me? "She has to lose," said Jazz, shrugging her shoulders. "She has to. To win means an impossible future. You told her to lose. You said so?"

"Yes, she knows to lose. But even so…" I trailed off. Jazz must see how difficult it was going to be for her pony.

She stared down at the lane, not seeming to notice the biting wind in her sweater and jeans. "She has to lose," she repeated to herself, like a mantra.

Suddenly, it all kicked off. The group of men became alert, their attention on the approaching horses. The sound of hooves on asphalt cut through the air, and Jazz, her dog, and I all turned, focusing on the scene unfolding below us.

Who would appear around the bend first?

The clatter of hoofbeats, louder every second, was joined by the sound of jingling harness, of wheels spinning on asphalt, of men's voices urging on the horses. I felt my throat tighten with dread—I didn't want to see Falling Snow straining to win or, even worse, being beaten along because she was not winning. I wanted to screw up my eyes and put my hands over my ears to shut out the pain and sweat and terror approaching. But I couldn't. I had to see. Like a horror film where it was too horrible to watch, yet unbearable not to, I had to know whether Falling Snow would win or lose. Either outcome was going to be painful—for Snow, for Jazz, and now for me.

Jazz stood silent, her violet eyes betraying nothing, her face like stone, one hand on her trembling dog's head.

Three horses pulling sulkies burst into view. A skewbald and a roan were neck and neck, their manes flying like banners, their legs a blur. But there, too, was Falling Snow, her eyes wide and startled, her nostrils flaring with effort, her sides dark with sweat, foam from her mouth caught and blown by the wind. Her driver behind her slapped the slack of the reins on either side of her quarters, harder and harder, refusing to let her ease her pace, urging her to trot flat-out, forcing her faster and faster, shouting even as she gave her all.

She wasn't losing.

Falling Snow was in front of the skewbald and the roan.

Falling Snow was going to win.

The noise of the horses and the drivers drowned out the cheers and moans of the waiting crowd of travelers.

There was never any chance of Jazz's pony being allowed to choose her pace. Her driver was relentless. Falling Snow swept past the crowd a length in front of the other horses, and I turned, appalled, to her owner behind me.

Jazz buried her face in her hands as her pony trotted on, her driver whooping in victory. A sob like a wild animal escaped her as she fell to her knees, distraught. The dog whined, licking his mistress's hands, which covered her face.

Instinctively, I took a step toward Jazz, but the dog turned and growled at me, stopping me in my tracks.

"Jazz?" I said urgently. "Jazz, are you all right?"

The girl stood up shakily, leaning on her dog. I could see tear trails glistening on her cheeks, and her eyes flashed dangerously as she whispered something murderous under her breath, then louder, so that I could hear her.

"I'll never let this happen to you again," she vowed shakily, staring at her pony as the laughing lad seated on the sulky turned her roughly around with one rein, slapping her again to make her canter back to the crowd. "I'll die first."

And then she turned to me, her voice trembling but under control, only her clenched hands betraying her distress and new determination.

"Snow couldn't do it. She hadn't the strength. But I have. I have to be strong for both of us. I can do that. I will do that."

"What are you going to do?" I asked her, my heart pounding.

Jazz watched as the men surrounded her pony, laughing and exchanging money. I felt a shiver run up and down my spine, and I remembered the first time I saw her and how ghostlike she had seemed. Pale and determined, she seemed spiritual again.

"I won't let this happen again." She whispered, looking down at her pony, "I'll hide you Snow, I'll take care of you."

"But where will you go?" I asked. Where could a young girl and her pony—and presumably her dog, I couldn't imagine it letting Jazz out of its sight—disappear to?

"I'm not afraid," said Jazz, looking at me again. "I know how to survive. We'll lay low until it is time for everyone to leave this place. The *Armaya* will begin soon, but I won't be there to see it. We will go."

"Where will you go?" I repeated, thinking she might have family she could stay with. It seemed Jazz didn't think like that.

"I shall hide. With Snow and Kasali. We'll be free."

"But *where* will you hide?" I asked her.

Jazz turned and looked at me, her violet eyes burning into my soul. "You know places here. You tell me where I can hide."

For a second I thought Jazz wanted to come and stay at my house. But then I realized that wasn't what she meant at all. She needed somewhere to stay with Snow and her dog. Where on earth could a girl, her dog, and her pony hide? It was impossible!

"But the police will find you. They'll search and find you for sure," I said.

Jazz laughed. "You think my father would ask the police for help? He would rather die first! No, I just need somewhere to lay low. If I travel, my father will find me, that's certain. He has friends who will help him. How about where Drummer lives? Would that be a place where we could hide?"

This was madness—and I could just imagine the reception Jazz and her two dependants would get at the yard. I shook my head. As I did so, I felt Jazz stiffen, and she lifted her chin defiantly.

"So, you won't help us. I understand."

"No, I mean, I want to, I just can't think of anywhere. Let me think," I heard myself saying.

"Then I'll wait for you to decide where," said Jazz. To Jazz, my words were a promise, not a plea for some thinking time, which was how I had intended them. With horror, I realized I was now responsible for hiding a girl, a pony, and a dog.

"I shall meet you here tomorrow, at this same time," said Jazz. "We will be ready to go. I cannot stay longer, the *Armaya* will soon begin."

I felt a tightness in my chest. How could Jazz possibly make it alone? How could I possibly find her a sanctuary? And what was this *Armaya* she was going on about? I asked her, and her reply made the hairs on the back of my neck stand up.

"A curse," Jazz replied, her eyes like steel. "I have cursed my father. It is done. Until tomorrow…" And with that

Jazz and her dog turned and ran off through the trees, leaving me shocked and shivering on the hillside.

CHAPTER 9

I COULDN'T KEEP MY BIG mouth shut. When I told Katy and Bean about the race, they were appalled—but not in the way I thought they would be.

"How could you go and watch?" asked Katy. "How could you possibly want to see those poor horses?"

"I had to find out whether Falling Snow won or not, don't you get it?" I replied.

"I don't see how you can be friendly with the girl if she allows her pony to be raced like that," said Bean.

"But she loves Falling Snow, that's the point—" I began.

"Well, she's got a funny way of showing it," Katy snapped.

"I'd never let anyone do that to Tiffany," declared Bean. "I just wouldn't."

"Her father doesn't sound like the sort of person she could reason with!" I said. "Jazz didn't *want* her pony to race, and she wanted her to lose it so she wouldn't have to race again."

I couldn't understand what they didn't get about the situation. It was as though they were deliberately misunderstanding or that I was talking in a different language. I kept telling them how Jazz loved Falling Snow and didn't want her to race, but Katy and Bean seemed determined to hear the complete opposite. I had to make them understand.

I tried again. "Jazz swore she wouldn't let her father race Snow again," I said earnestly. "She *cried!*"

"A bit late now," Bean retorted heartlessly. "She should have done all that before."

"She's going to run away," I said, my voice getting louder. I was starting to lose control—it was so frustrating. "She's put a curse on her father, that's how much she hates him for hurting Snow. Can you imagine running away? How can you doubt how much she cares for Snow?"

"I bet she doesn't," said Bean. "I was always threatening to run away whenever my sisters were horrible to me about my riding lessons. I got as far as the end of the road once, with some cookies and a peanut butter and jelly sandwich tied up in a handkerchief on the end of a broom handle. I'd packed all my toy ponies in a duffel bag, too."

"Did you?" asked Katy, impressed. "What happened?"

"Oh, some nosy old woman at the end of the road saw me and called my mom, and she ran after me. I was only six."

"This is a bit different. Jazz isn't six, and she's going to take Falling Snow with her. She's serious!"

"They're all the same, the travelers," insisted Katy. "They just tie up their ponies then race them hard. I don't see why we should believe your friend's any different."

I had the feeling I was pushing a boulder up a hill. The harder I pushed, the heavier it became and threatened to come back down and crush me. I had hoped my friends might help me think of where Jazz could hide away, but now I couldn't bring myself to tell them that part. I had a terrible feeling that because of the way the conversation had gone, not only would they refuse to help, but they might actually give Jazz away.

Then things got worse. Cat and James arrived. Together. James stopped and spoke to us—Cat smiled and said hello to Katy and Bean but totally ignored me. Which I didn't mind at all. It's always worse when she sneers or makes stupid, cutting remarks or calls me Mia instead of Pia. She thinks that's hilarious.

"What's new?" James grinned. We were all still smarting from our disagreement, and the air was thick with tension.

"The travelers are still around," said Katy, glaring at me. "Still racing their horses, still cluttering up the Sloping Field."

James frowned. "Moth's been on edge all week," he said. "It's as though she knows they're here. I wish they'd go."

"Perhaps if a certain person didn't keep making them feel welcome, they would," remarked Cat, giving me the evil eye. Katy and Bean looked uncomfortable. James picked up on it, of course.

"What do you mean?" he asked Cat.

"*Mia's* new friend was at the yard the other day."

Oh, seven kinds of hell, I thought. Cat had seen Jazz. And another, terrible thought struck me. If she had seen us talking, had she also seen…?

"I bet she was casing the joint so she and her sort can come back for a raid," continued Cat. "I bet nothing's safe, the tack, the ponies. She had a good look at Moth, walked right up to her as bold as you like, and peered into her stable!"

Yes, she had.

James looked at me with a mixture of disbelief and astonishment. I sighed.

"It wasn't like that. Jazz wanted my help to communicate with her pony. She was only here a few minutes."

"What about Moth?" exploded James.

So not the reaction I was looking for. This thing with Jazz was getting totally out of hand.

"Well, she did go up to Moth, but it wasn't at all like Cat says, it really wasn't..." I trailed off. It was hopeless trying to explain.

"I don't understand you, Pia," said James, shaking his head. "What are you thinking of? I know you weren't here when I got Moth, you didn't see how she was, but by being friendly with the travelers, it's as though you're betraying Moth. It's as though you're betraying all of us."

I stood with my mouth open. This was so unfair!

"I didn't invite her!" I shouted. "I didn't tell her where I keep Drum, she just turned up! What am I supposed to do, ignore her? Refuse to help her? What would you do?"

"That depends on where your loyalties lie," said Cat. "With the travelers or with us. Maybe you're a homeless traveler yourself!"

I stormed off. I was so angry! Everyone seemed to be blaming me for the travelers' very existence, and Cat was so taking advantage of the situation and making it work for her. It wasn't fair. I knew Jazz loved Falling Snow the same way I loved Drummer, the same way Bean, Katy, James, and even Cat loved their ponies. Why wouldn't anyone see that?

No one came after me. It wasn't like the soaps on TV—if it had been, James would have caught up with me and sworn his undying support, assuring me that even though he didn't fully understand my motives, he'd trust I was doing the right thing.

Well, this wasn't a TV soap opera. This was real life, and I was busy falling out with my new friends. I didn't even need Catriona's help to do that—I managed to do a pretty good job all by myself. I could imagine how thrilled she must be.

I went where I always go when I'm upset and I need some help to sort out the problems of life (which seem far too frequent!). My gorgeous bay pony looked up from his hay net as I closed the stable door behind me.

"Uh-oh, you look like you've got to spend the day with Skinny Lynny," he remarked.

"I'm the enemy, apparently," I told him miserably, leaning against the wall.

"What have you done now?" asked Drum, still chewing.

"It's Jazz. No one seems to understand that she's not some pony-beating lunatic who wants to steal all the saddles."

"Well, you don't know that she doesn't want to steal the saddles," said Drum.

"Oh, don't you start!"

"OK, then get out of my stable," said Drum.

I sighed. I didn't want to fight with Drummer, too. "OK, you have a point," I agreed grudgingly. "But Jazz loves Snow, you know *that*."

"Yup!"

"So how can I persuade the others?"

"Why are you even bothering?"

"What? Do you think I shouldn't help Jazz?"

"That's one option—or you could help her and just not tell anyone."

I was going to reply to this, but stopped with my mouth half open, letting Drummer's words of pony wisdom sink in.

"Why don't you just shut up about her and do your own thing?" Drum continued. "You're asking for trouble, going on about it, aren't you?"

I thought furiously, digesting Drum's words. My head hurt a bit.

"Is that—" I struggled for the word. "Honest?"

"It's smart!" retorted Drum.

I had to agree that it was. Why was I going on about Jazz? It made sense to say nothing. Or—my thoughts raced on—I could simply stay away from Jazz and Falling Snow. I mean, what had I been thinking, going along to watch the race? I didn't have to go back tomorrow. It had nothing to do with me, did it? I couldn't help it if she'd misunderstood me. Putting it all on me wasn't my idea, it was hers, and I had no idea where Jazz could hide out. What was I, a real estate agent for runaways? It wasn't like

I could make a difference—Jazz's dad was in charge, and we were both powerless. The more I thought about it, the more it made sense.

"Well?" said Drummer, fixing his big brown eyes on me. He was still chewing—I couldn't imagine a drama big enough to make my pony actually stop eating. The world could stop, hell could freeze over, birds could turn pink and fall out of the sky, and through it all I'd still hear the sound of Drum's teeth grinding away on his hay. But then, I remembered, the drama was all mine, not Drum's.

"Good plan!" I told him, nodding. "I'll forget about Jazz and her pony. Perfect!" Yes, it was, I decided. That was that. Definitely. Done deal.

"There's just one problem," said Drum.

"No, there isn't," I replied, shaking my head, not wanting to hear it.

"She's relying on you to help her."

"But I don't know anywhere she can hide," I wailed. "And even if I did…"

"What?" said Drummer, turning to face me. "If you did, what would you do?"

I didn't know. I didn't want to think about it. I wanted my life to be as it was before Jazz and the travelers had arrived. Before James hated me and I'd seen how Moth and Drummer had behaved with Jazz, before it had complicated my relationship with everyone at the yard.

"Oh, they'll be gone soon," I said, storming out and

closing Drummer's door. "And then we can all get back to normal!"

"OK!" mumbled Drummer. "If you say so."

I almost believed it.

CHAPTER 10

SO THAT'S ALL *I have to do*, I thought, pedaling furiously out of the yard gates and turning toward home. I just side with everyone at the yard, agree that the travelers—including Jazz—are a pain in the neck, and stay away from her. It wasn't as if I had the perfect hideaway lined up. Phew.

It would be easy, I thought as I got to the bottom of the hill and turned right past the old factory. The factory, I remembered, where the boys who had tormented poor Moth had lived. Poor tethered Moth, who hadn't been able to get away.

After all, I decided as I braked at the crosswalk to let a woman and a child cross, Jazz was nothing to me, was she?

Also, I reminded myself as I turned into my road, slowing down as I reached our tiny cottage, if Jazz wanted to run away then that was her business. How did I get involved, anyway? Oh, yes, I remembered, Epona's magic touch and my big mouth. A lethal combination, as ever! Well, Jazz's problems had nothing to do with me.

So why couldn't I stop thinking about her? Why did I feel that I was letting her down by turning my back on her? Why did it feel like I was abandoning her? What was it about Jazz that fascinated me? It was as though she held the same power over me as she did over the ponies.

Darn it!

I let myself in through the front door and yelled. Mom was home, and I could smell something delicious cooking, which was a change in these times of her getting fit. Good. A heavy dose of normality was what I needed. All this inner turmoil was making me hungry.

"Ah, hello, honey," said Mom, an apron on over a little black number she'd managed to squeeze back into since embarking on her gym-fest. She was scooping some brown goo into a glass bowl.

"I hate to do this to you, Pia, but any chance of you watching TV in your room this evening? Jerry's coming for dinner—I'm cooking," she added, aiming a wry grin in my direction.

"Oh, all right," I mumbled. "What's on the menu?"

"Well, I've made this chocolate mousse for dessert—no fat, apart from what's in the chocolate—and we're having steak and salad before that."

"No, I mean what's for *my* dinner?" I asked.

"Oh. Well, I know you don't like steak, so I got you some pasta. OK?"

"No chocolate mousse for me? I could use something to cheer me up." Typical! No welcome distraction from my inner turmoil there.

"What's up?" said Mom.

"Huh? Oh, nothing," I said. I didn't think Mom needed to know about me fraternizing with traveler folk. Things were awkward enough without her overreacting like grown-ups do when they don't know the full story.

"In that case, eat your pasta and buzz off!" Mom told me with a grin, licking chocolate mousse off the spoon with a look of guilty glee on her face. "Jerry will be here any minute, and I can't have you cramping my style!"

"You shouldn't have led him to believe that you're too young to have a daughter my age!" I teased her. What are things coming to when I'm forced upstairs so that my mom can entertain her boyfriend? And why hadn't I been offered the chocolate mousse spoon? I gobbled down the pasta, made Mom promise to save me some chocolate mousse, and galloped upstairs.

Throwing myself on my bed with a sigh, I looked up at my calendar. It's a really nice one with a different horse on each month—and October was a stunning chestnut with a white blaze in a desert. The day after tomorrow was Monday, the first day of our mid-semester break, hooray! Our school breaks the year into quarters. Except that Monday and Tuesday were circled, and I'd written in red felt tip "*Two days of hell!*" And I wasn't kidding either, because I was due to waste it by staying with my dad and his horrible girlfriend, Skinny Lynny. For a whole two days!

Triple pooh.

At least that meant I would be out of Jazz's way, I thought. It seemed I was going to be the one running away.

I went to bed, the occasional bursts of laughter coming from downstairs preventing me from going to sleep, and then still unable to drift off when the bursts stopped and it all went quiet. I didn't want to think about what my mom and Jerry might have been doing then, but anyway, I couldn't stop thinking about Jazz and Falling Snow and how they were both depending on me. Unfairly, I thought, when I still hadn't been able to magically pull the ultimate hiding place out of thin air.

But I must have drifted off in the end because suddenly I woke up with a start. It was pitch-black, I didn't know what time it was, and the solution to where Jazz could hide had suddenly (annoyingly!) popped into my mind of its own accord. It was blindingly obvious.

Oh, wow, I thought, *of course*. No one will ever find her there!

But that meant I had no excuse not to help Jazz.

Pooh.

So I lay there and had a conscience struggle, mentally listing all the "fors" and "againsts" about revealing my hide-out. Helping Snow and helping Jazz and doing the right thing came under the "fors," and staying close with my friends at the yard came under "againsts." And now I had the perfect hiding place, which was the biggest "for" of all.

Four "fors" and only one "against."

So that settled it. I was helping Jazz after all. End of story!

CHAPTER 11

THE WEATHER THE NEXT day was more winter than autumn. The wind blew in gusts, undecided about which direction it wanted to come from and go to, making Drummer's long coat stand to attention one minute, then lie flat like it had been ironed the next. We stood on the hillside, unable to turn our backs to the ever changing wind, hoping the driving rain wouldn't get any heavier. The weather threw up strange sounds that made me jumpy. I kept thinking someone was watching us, spying on us. I was glad I had Drum to talk to.

I had put Drummer's waterproof exercise sheet on him to keep his back dry, but the wind kept getting underneath it and lifting it up like a kite—only the fillet string under his tail stopped it from sweeping us both along like a sailboat. The situation was not one taken stoically by Drum.

"Couldn't you have picked a less exposed meeting place?" he grumbled. "Like the top of Mount Everest or the middle of the North Pole? And this fillet string keeps getting caught under my tail. It's most uncomfortable!"

"Goodness, how you do complain," I replied, wishing I'd put another fleece on.

"What made you decide to help our traveler friend, anyway?" asked Drum.

"You did," I replied, wanting to blame someone. "I know reverse psychology when I hear it."

"I knew this would be my fault," he mumbled.

I patted his neck. "You want to help Jazz and Falling Snow, you can't fool me." I swallowed hard. The next sentence wasn't going to be easy. "I know you love Jazz, and you don't want Snow to race again. You like to come across as hard, Drummer, but I know you better than that."

Drummer tossed his head and snorted. I couldn't tell whether it was a yes snort or a no snort. Strangely, I felt better. Saying that my pony loved Jazz had been hard, but it felt better to get it out in the open. I wondered, if it came to it and Drum had to make a choice, whether he would stay with me or go with Jazz. I put that thought to the back of my mind. I'd decided on my course of action, and whatever I did wouldn't make Jazz any less of a pony whisperer—a real one.

A noise behind us made us whirl around in fright. All this cloak-and-dagger stuff was making both our nerves bad.

"You came," Jazz said simply. "I didn't think you would."

Oh, pooh, I thought. Jazz hadn't expected me to be there—she hadn't been relying on me at all, and I could have stayed away without it being a big deal! Jazz sat astride Falling Snow, a folded blanket under her legs. She wore a big jacket over her sweater and jeans. Her dog, as always, stood by her side, panting, his amber eyes staring at me.

"Come on," I said, turning Drum into the wood.

I wanted to get this over with and prayed no one would see us together.

I led the way through the woods, back toward the yard, skirting around it so that we didn't go too close. Riding around three of the farmer's fields and keeping out of sight close to the trees, we headed for the lake, the land dropping as we rode through the trees. Bare branches stretched skyward like skinny fingers, reaching for the light.

Past the lake we went, the ponies' hooves sinking into the mud at the bottom of the hill, and started to climb upward again. It was a long way from the travelers' camp at the Sloping Field and, eventually, I pushed through thick rhododendron bushes overgrowing the path and came to a halt in a small clearing. Jazz nudged Falling Snow up beside Drummer.

"This is a good place," she said, looking around. The wind was quieter here, and we were cocooned by trees, evergreen rhododendron bushes, and dense holly. It felt protected and hidden. Secret.

Dismounting, I walked toward the center of the clearing, leading Drummer to the far side of a grassy mound, as tall as a man. Falling Snow followed, and I noticed Jazz's eyes widen when she saw an old wooden door embedded into the mound. Arched, it had huge iron hinges and a handle. The wood, although mossy and old, was still solid and sound.

Jazz slid off her pony and examined the door. "What is this?" she asked me, puzzled.

"It's an old icehouse," I explained. "It's been here for

years and years, but not many people know about it. It's where the owners of the big house used to store ice from the lake in the winter for use in the summer."

"What big house?" asked Jazz, looking around.

"It's fallen down, gone," I said. "I couldn't open the door last time I was here, but I'm hoping our combined strength will shift it." I knew it did open because James had told me he'd been inside the icehouse.

We both grasped hold of the huge, iron, circular handle and pulled. For a while, nothing happened, then we felt it move.

"Oh, we can do it!" I exclaimed, strangely excited and scared at the same time. The icehouse gave me the creeps, but Jazz didn't seem worried, and I didn't want to seem like a wuss in front of her. Ignoring my feeling of dread, I concentrated on gathering my strength.

We pulled again, kicking the mud away from the base of the door to make it easier. And it did open, reluctantly, creakily, spookily, revealing a dark emptiness inside.

Pulling out the flashlight I'd brought with me, I switched it on, and we peered into the gloom. Dark, damp brick walls disappeared into nothing.

"I'll look," said Jazz, taking the flashlight and walking inside.

I stood outside in the daylight. Nothing would have persuaded me to take a step inside that place. It smelled musty and old. It was damp, dark, and dingy. It felt like a tomb. *It is madness*, I thought, *Jazz can't stay here*. A hole buried in a grass mound wasn't my idea of a great place to shack up for a night or two. But in all other respects, the icehouse had seemed the perfect place for Jazz to hide: it was tucked away, it would keep her out of the wind and rain, and there was grass around it for Falling Snow.

But now I wasn't so sure. I couldn't even begin to imagine being in the icehouse at night, with the wind playing in the trees and every sound suggesting ghosts and who knows what else! Surely now Jazz would give up her idea of running away.

"Not exactly the Ritz, is it?" snorted Drummer.

"If you've got any other ideas, I'm all ears!" I told him. I mean, it's all very well being critical, but it wasn't like my pony had volunteered any input, was it?

"I'm just saying…" said Drum, nibbling grass off the top of the mound.

Jazz returned with the flashlight. Her face said it all.

"I take it you'd rather not stay here," I said. I didn't have a plan B, so if plan A was out of the question, then that was it!

"I can stay here…" she said slowly. She seemed distracted.

"I'm sensing there's a *but* coming," I said.

"There is something…"

"What?"

"Something about this place, this icehouse."

"Yeah, it's really spooky!" I said, shivering.

"Something bad has happened here."

"Give the girl a peanut!" exclaimed Drummer. "I could have told you that!"

What did she have to go and say that for? The place was spooky enough. It didn't need any more drama. And what did Drummer mean? He could have said something sooner. I gulped. Suddenly, my mouth felt very dry.

"How bad?" I asked. My voice sounded a bit croaky.

"It feels, it feels…" Jazz hesitated, putting her hand on the inner wall of the icehouse. "It has the feel of a…"

I so didn't want to ask the question. I so had to.

"A what?"

"A tomb."

"Got it in one!" interjected Drummer.

"Can you just leave it, please Drum?" I said.

"OK, OK, suit yourself!" said Drummer huffily. A tomb. Oh, is that all? I had thought that myself. I didn't welcome Jazz agreeing with me. Could she really tell or was she just being melodramatic? Was it just an excuse not to stay?

"*Okaaaay!*" I said slowly, glancing around. "So, then this is a no-no. I don't have anywhere else I can show you. No second choice, I'm afraid."

"This will be fine," said Jazz, switching off the flashlight and dumping her bag on the ground. "Whatever occurred here happened a long, long time ago."

Did that matter? I thought. I wouldn't stay in the ice-house overnight if you paid me a million bucks. I wasn't sure I'd even volunteer to hang around in daylight now.

"You mean, you'll stay here?" I said, appalled.

"Yes, until my father moves on."

"But…but…aren't you…*scared?*"

Jazz laughed. "No, I'm not scared. Spirits are all around us, all the time. I'm not frightened to stay here."

"But you'll freeze!" I said, trying to find some excuse for her to abandon her plan.

"Kasali will keep me warm." Jazz patted her dog. The dog's tail almost wagged. He licked her hand.

"What's it like inside?" I asked.

"There's enough room for me," said Jazz. "The entrance falls away into a huge pit with steps down. The door is strong, and it will keep out the rain. Can I keep this?" Jazz lifted the flashlight.

I nodded, knowing that Jazz wouldn't be able to keep it on all night. I couldn't imagine sitting in the icehouse in total darkness, even with Kasali. Imagine the spiders! Imagine…I shuddered. Then I had a thought.

"You can have Drum's exercise sheet to lie on if you like," I offered, unfastening Drum's girth and pulling the sheet out from under his saddle. "It's waterproof."

"That's generous of you!" exclaimed Drum indignantly. "I mean, don't ask or anything. Just feel free to give my stuff away to anyone!"

"You'll be OK, and you won't have to put up with the fillet string," I whispered to him. I knew he didn't mind.

Jazz took the sheet gratefully. It would make a difference.

"Here." Jazz pressed something into my hand. It was two ten-dollar bills. I gasped. I didn't expect payment. But I had jumped to the wrong conclusion.

"I'll need some food," she said. "I couldn't take anything

from home. As far as my dad's concerned, I've just gone for a ride."

"But I can't!" I heard myself say. I didn't dare tell Jazz that I was going to stay with my own father for two days.

A pair of vivid violet eyes bored into me as Jazz frowned. "I only have a chocolate bar and a small bottle of water," Jazz said. "I thought you were going to help me."

I chewed the inside of my mouth. I hadn't signed up to helping Jazz for life. What did she expect? But then, how did I expect her to survive? She could hardly run down to the supermarket and push a shopping cart full of groceries back to the icehouse, could she? Why was everything always more complicated than I expected? Clearly, I hadn't thought this through.

I nodded. "I'll figure something out," I heard myself say. I could go to the Quickmart near the stables, but how was I going to get my purchases to Jazz?

"What will your dog eat?" I asked.

Jazz laughed. "Kasali will make himself known to the local rabbit population!" She laughed even more when I made a face.

"What does *Kasali* mean?" I asked.

"Forest Spirit," Jazz replied, fondling her dog's ears. Kasali licked her hand before returning his gaze to me, full of distrust, guarding his mistress. No wonder Jazz wasn't scared.

As I mounted Drummer, Jazz put her hand on Drummer's neck. My pony turned and nuzzled her, just as Moth had. I swallowed hard as I felt my stomach churn.

"Thank you," Jazz said quietly. "I know you won't let me down."

I couldn't hang around—I had my two days of hell to get started. As I turned Drummer for home, the trees and bushes closed in on Jazz's hiding place, shutting us out. *It really is the perfect place to go if you don't want to be found,* I thought.

At least I'd got that right.

CHAPTER 12

I SPENT MOST OF MONDAY morning getting lost in the new house my dad shares with Skinny Lynny. It's much bigger than the one me and Mom live in 'cause my dad's got a good job and so has Lynn (that's how he met Skinny, she works with him). It's one of those so-called "executive homes" in a new subdivision, each one looking exactly the same as its next-door neighbor.

When I'd arrived on Sunday night, I'd dumped my suitcase in my bedroom with its private bathroom—which was quite exciting—while Skinny had insisted on telling me all about the new decor and furnishings she'd had put in. Lots of animal-print cushions, flower canvases on the wall, and glass tables. It looked like one of those made-over houses on TV.

Anyway, I'd made all the right noises as I'd traipsed behind Skinny whose tiny backside was poured into skintight jeans. Her long, straightened blonde hair reached almost to her waist, and she jangled as she walked, adorned with many bangles and necklaces, giving her a sound track like bad plumbing.

"I've just finished the guest bedroom," Skinny had said with a flourish as she'd swung open the door, and I oohed and ahhed in all the right places. It turned out she hadn't finished it at all, she hadn't even started it—just chosen colors and fabrics and ordered the decorator about.

The kitchen had a huge stainless steel range cooker, so I expected great things in the eating department. Cue big disappointment: it turned out that Skinny doesn't cook—probably because she doesn't eat. My dad does what cooking there is, and the range was barely troubled all through my visit. We ate out most of the time, which at least made a change from the lettuce leaves and cherry tomato regime with Mom.

Of course, all I kept thinking about was Jazz, and the problem of getting supplies to her. As I'd ridden home from the icehouse on Sunday, I realized I'd have to recruit an accomplice. But who?

Not James. His Cat connection put him firmly out of the running, not to mention Moth's past.

Not Katy. She would have been my first choice, but she had been so against the travelers, I couldn't risk it.

Not Dee-Dee. Too occupied with her Horse of the Year Show preparations.

Not Bean.

Why not Bean? I had thought. She at least had shown the tiniest sympathy toward Jazz's plight.

Bean. Mmmm. I hadn't had time to think about it for long as I had to go to Dad's right away. I'd asked Drummer's opinion.

"Yup, call in Bean," he'd agreed. "She's ditzy, but her heart's in the right place."

Getting Bean on her own hadn't been easy—everyone seemed to be at the yard. Eventually, though, I'd cornered her outside Drummer's stable and had whispered my problem to her.

It had actually been easier than I'd thought because once Bean knew Jazz had actually done what she had threatened to do and run away to help her pony, she totally changed her mind about her.

"She must love her pony to do that!" she'd said, her eyebrows disappearing into her bangs, obviously impressed. "I mean, I never thought she actually would do it!"

"But I told you she was going to," I'd replied a bit testily.

"Yes, but I thought you were just being dramatic to get us on her side. What would happen if she hadn't run away?"

We'd fallen silent at this point as Catriona walked across the yard to Bambi's stable, forcing us to take advantage of a lull in tack room activity and retreat into there and whisper some more.

"Jazz's father will race Falling Snow again," I'd said. "As she's so fast, Jazz is scared he'll sell her like he sold Snow's mother."

"But Falling Snow belongs to Jazz, doesn't she?" Bean had asked, confused.

"Yes." I'd sighed. "But Jazz says that doesn't matter. Her father will sell her anyway."

"I suppose it's like our ponies," Bean had mused. "I mean, my parents say Tiffany is my pony, but they bought her, and they pay for her keep. She's not legally mine. They could do the same—sell her at the drop of a hat. Actually," she'd murmured, "they wouldn't need much persuading."

I'd never seen Bean's parents at the stables. Everyone else gets dropped off by their mom or dad, but Bean cycles, like me.

"Aren't your parents interested in Tiffany?" I'd asked her.

"Nah. They're far more into my sisters' interests—Haley plays the violin, and Grace paints. But then, my mom sculpts, and my dad's a musician, so they're all into the arts. I'm the black sheep of the family. I think they bought me Tiff so they could get on with being all artistic without me hanging around, not getting it. It's like I'm from another planet. Hey! Maybe that's it! I've been sent down to Earth and planted with a human family!"

I couldn't help thinking how many times we'd all thought that very same thing—that Bean was from another planet. How strange that her whole family was so different from Bean. It was the first time she'd mentioned them. It certainly explained why I'd never seen them at the yard. Horses were obviously not a subject they could relate to, any more than Bean was into their interests.

I'd impressed upon her the need for total secrecy: "You have to swear you won't tell a soul where Jazz is hiding. No one. Not Katy or James or ANYONE!"

I knew she wouldn't because instead of just saying, "Of course I won't," Bean had pursed her lips and weighed up the pros and cons before solemnly swearing that she'd rather die first. So I'd told her where Jazz was, and she'd gone all wide-eyed when I explained about the icehouse and had agreed to look in on Jazz later that afternoon and again on Tuesday, taking her more water and food. I'd given her Jazz's money.

"I'll take some dog biscuits, too," she'd volunteered. "We've got some in our garage from when my grand-mother came to stay. She's got a West Highland terrier," she'd added, when I'd given her a look. I'd thought dog biscuits were a strange diet for an old lady, even one related to Bean.

And then at that moment, Catriona had waltzed in. "Dog biscuits?" she'd asked. "Who wants dog biscuits?"

"I've adopted a dog at the local dog rescue," Bean had lied, calm as you like. "It's only five bucks a year, but I'm going to see if I can do more to help. Interested in donating something, Cat?" she'd added.

"Wow!" I'd said, after Cat had gone. "I'm impressed!"

"Sometimes a girl has to think on her feet," Bean had replied, and I'd congratulated myself on my choice of accomplice.

It had been so easy to get Bean on Jazz's side once she knew Jazz was serious about her pony's welfare and had taken her into hiding, I'd wondered whether the others would feel the same way, but I didn't dare tell anyone else. The fewer people who knew where Jazz was, the bet-ter, and besides, Bean was looking after Drummer for me while I was away, so including her in the Jazz escapade made things neat. I could also get any news when I rang her to ask about Drum, avoiding suspicion on the yard if anyone overheard. The plan had seemed to slide into place quite well.

I hadn't wanted to think about how Jazz was going to react when Bean turned up at her so-called secret hiding place instead of me. I'd let Bean handle that one. It was a step too far for me; my courage seemed to have run its course. Also, I hoped Jazz wouldn't mention the feeling she had about someone having died there—that would freak Bean out big-time. I could just imagine it. She'd been worse than me at that séance. I could imagine Bean gallop-ing home and never going back.

It soon became obvious that Dad and Skinny had planned my visit with military precision, which was fine by me. If I'd been asked to make a list of all the things I'd like to do with my dad and Skinny, sitting around making small talk would be at the very bottom of a very, very tiny piece of paper.

"We're going out this afternoon, Pumpkin," Dad an-nounced. When was I going to tackle him about my stupid pet name? "To Harrisburg House."

"It's a fabulous old house with a walled garden. Built in the eighteenth century," explained Skinny, sipping some warm water in which floated a thin slice of lemon, like a leaf floats on a puddle.

"Full of history!" exclaimed Dad, rubbing his hands to-gether. "We thought we'd get a bit of culture today!"

"And there's the most divine café on site, with a wonderful shop," added Skinny, running her hand through her hair so that it stood away from her face, showing off her cheekbones.

"OK," I said, wishing I was at the yard with Drummer. I was destined instead for Harrisburg House and its shop.

We piled into the car—me in the back, of course. We hadn't got halfway out of the drive when my cell phone rang.

It was Bean.

"Hello?" I said, in hushed tones. I could see Skinny gawking at me in the rearview mirror. Nosy!

"I've been to see Jazz!" Bean said. "She wasn't very friendly, and that dog of hers is like a wolf. I thought he was going to rip me to pieces!"

"Ahhh. Mmmm," I said. Well, I couldn't say much more with Dad and Skinny straining to hear.

"She kept saying no one else was supposed to know and that she didn't need my help, even though she had no food and hardly any water. Talk about ungrateful! Anyway, she wanted to know whether her family had upped and left, but I told her they were still rooted to the Sloping Field. I don't know how long she's intending to stay at the IH hotel."

"I see," I said.

"Tiff went, well, weird when we were there," continued Bean. "I thought she'd be all *wahhhh*, like she usually is, but she went freakishly calm and kept dragging me over to Jazz like she was a bucket of feed. Really weird!"

Not really, I thought, remembering how Drummer and Moth had been with Jazz.

"Are you all right?"

"Er, well, it's a bit tricky right now," I said, hoping Bean would somehow buck the trend of being on a different wavelength to everyone else and get my problem. Wonder of wonders, she did!

"Is someone listening to us?" she said dramatically.

"Absolutely!" I said.

"Oh, OK. Well, I thought you'd want to know that everything's going according to plan here, so don't worry. Drummer's fine, too. He's out in the field with Bluey because he's lost a shoe."

"But he was only shod last week!" I exclaimed.

"No, not Drummer, Bluey," Bean explained. "Bluey's lost a shoe. The farrier's coming this afternoon. Oh, by the way, do you know what a black mark on a white sock is called?"

"An ermine mark," I volunteered. "Why?"

"Oh, nothing. Call me later when you're alone."

"Will do," I agreed, ending the call. Phew! Bean seemed to have everything under control, which made a change. I looked up to see Skinny Lynny smirking at me.

"What?" I asked.

"It's OK, Pia, if you want to talk to your boyfriend, we won't listen."

For a moment, I wondered what on earth she was going on about, but then I remembered how, ages ago, a difficult moment with James had been explained by the assumption that he was my boyfriend. *Huh*, I thought, *if you only knew!*

Obviously she had been listening—even if she had got it totally wrong. I slumped down in the seat and looked out of the car window as we sped past fields. I love seeing how many horses I can spot on a car journey. By the time we reached Harrisburg House. I'd spotted two grays, a chestnut, and a bay that looked a bit like Drummer, only with two white legs. Oh, and a llama, but that didn't count.

Harrisburg House was big and ugly and full of old furniture and paintings of dead people. (I don't mean they'd been painted after they'd died, I mean they'd died years ago, after the portraits had been finished.) There was one of a woman on a dappled gray. She was riding sidesaddle in a gorgeous blue habit, which reminded me of Epona. My little stone statue of the Roman and Celtic goddess sitting sideways on her horse was zipped into my bag. I didn't dare leave her anywhere, and besides, I never knew when I might happen across a horse and a conversation would be needed.

"Isn't this fireplace just so elegant, Paul?" enthused Skinny, running her hand along the huge marble surround. "Do you think we could have something similar in the living room?"

"It is lovely," agreed my dad.

It wasn't. It was hideous. I thought of our little fireplace in our house and was glad my mom and I lived there instead of my dad's rather soulless home. Thank goodness I didn't live with him and Skinny. I'd rather live with my mom any day—even with her crazy boyfriends. At least my mom's love life meant she didn't drag me off to do stuff all the time, instead leaving me to spend my life with Drummer.

We trooped from room to room, from libraries, to bedrooms, to the kitchens, to the cellars.

"Are there any stables?" I asked. There must have been, but I wanted to know whether they were still there.

"Yes, there are!" Skinny Lynny exclaimed. "They've turned them into the most fabulous café. We're going there next."

What a terrible thing to do to old stables, I thought. There ought to be a law against it. But actually, when we got to the coffee shop called, unimaginatively, the Old Coach House, I discovered they'd kept some of the old stalls intact, so we got our tray of coffees, Coke, salad (Skinny), burger (Dad), and lasagna (me) and sat inside an alcove created out of one of them. I could see the brass rings, which the carriage horses would have been tied to, and they even had the old trough. I wondered whether the old house that used to be near Laurel Farm had had fabulous old stables like these. How I would have loved to have seen them! Squirreling away most of the fancy misshapen brown and white sugar lumps on the table, I folded them up in a paper napkin and zipped them up in my bag with Epona for company. Drum would go crazy for those!

"Pia, if you've got a sweet tooth, we can buy you some sweets, rather than see you resort to stealing sugar from tables," offered Skinny Lynny. "But I have to say that sugar will not only rot your teeth, it will seriously compromise your figure."

"They're for Drummer, actually," I told her, making a face.

"Less of the attitude, Pia," Dad remarked, siding with Skinny.

I was itching to call Bean, but I couldn't get a moment to myself. Skinny even came with me when I went to the restroom, like we were best friends or something. After the café we walked around some more and went to the shop where Skinny bought some napkin rings. I bought a jar of gooseberry jam for Mom, and then re-membered she was on her health-food bender. It was too late by then. I'd parted with my cash. *Still*, I thought, *she is bound to get fed up with all the lettuce in the end and return to real food.*

As we walked back to the car, Dad and Skinny got lovey-dovey, holding hands and giggling. Skinny started tickling my dad, and my dad went all stupid and gooey-eyed with his trophy girlfriend. I trailed along behind trying not to watch and wishing they'd knock it off and grow up.

Finally, I got a second to myself when we got back home, and I called Bean for an update.

That didn't go as planned—Bean's phone was switched off. As I had only a half hour window because I was sup-posed to be getting ready to go out with Dad and Skinny for dinner, I couldn't wait and, in desperation, called Katy instead.

Big mistake. Katy was not her usual cool, calm, collected self.

"Pia! Oh, you won't believe what's been happening today!"

"What?" I asked, bracing myself for a long story about Bluey's lost shoe and possibly the oh-so-familiar tale of the farrier being late or not turning up at all or turning up and spending all the time on his cell instead of concentrating on shoeing Bluey.

"One of the travelers chased James and Cat when they were out riding! Actually ran after them!"

I caught my breath. This was so, so not good.

"Really?" I said, feeling a bit woozy.

"Yes, threatened them! Said his daughter was missing and that he knew someone was hiding her. Really crazy, he was. You know, demented."

My heart did a sort of horrible dance. I could just picture Jazz's father, some big, blustery, scary guy, scaring James and Cat, making the ponies tremble—especially poor Moth. Pooh, pooh, pooh.

"James shouted back at him apparently. That's when he chased them. Of course, he couldn't keep up with Moth and Bambi, but still, those travelers are just the pits! James says he's thinking of calling the police. How are you, anyway?" she said. "Having fun with your dad?"

"Er, not really. Is Bean around?"

"No, she's left for the evening. Should I tell her to call you?"

"No, no, it's OK. I'll text her. Can you give Drum a kiss for me?"

"Sure will. I can see him from here. He's twirling his hay net around like he does. Isn't he funny?"

"Yeah, when you don't have to spend half an hour the next day unraveling it," I told her.

I rattled off a text to Bean and went downstairs with a heavy heart. Things were going badly, and I still had another day to endure away from everything. I didn't know whether to be sad or glad. One thing was certain: there wasn't a thing I could do about it.

CHAPTER 13

I THOUGHT WE'D HAVE SOME girly fun today," said Skinny Lynny, smiling at me and my dad as she finished her coffee. "Pia and I will go shopping and get out of your hair, Paul—what's left of it!"

I glanced at my dad. I hadn't noticed, but he was going a bit thin on top. I bet he didn't like that! My heart sank—not because of my dad's disappearing hair, but because shopping with Skinny Lynny was last on my miniscule list of things I'd choose to do. Dad was all for it. He probably thought it would be a great bonding exercise.

I always have good intentions about being nice to Skinny Lynny, intentions which evaporate the moment I'm with her and her annoying little girl persona kicks in. I decided shopping might be the perfect opportunity to put those forgotten intentions into practice. A chance to check out the karma thing—you know, you get back what you put in, that sort of thing.

I'd managed to get a hold of Bean at about ten o'clock last night, and she'd confirmed Katy's story about Jazz's dad, making it sound even worse. There had been swearing, there had been threats. Bean was determined to visit Jazz again today, but she acknowledged that she needed to be extra careful. Meeting up with Jazz's irate father was the last thing she wanted to do. I couldn't help wondering whether Jazz's curse was starting to work. It did sound like her father had gone totally crazy.

Sitting at the kitchen table eating cornflakes with my dad and Skinny Lynny, I wished I had Drummer to talk to. I felt so out of everything and anxious about Jazz and Bean and James and everything. Not Cat. I didn't care much if Jazz's dad chased her. And now I was going shopping. *Whoop-de-doo*. I thought we'd go to some big shopping mall, but it turned out that Skinny's idea of shopping was very different to mine.

"We'll go to Fairview," she said as we got into her very red, very shiny car my dad had bought for her. The thought crossed my mind as to whether Skinny would be fed up with her car by the time I was old enough to drive. Would my dad pass it on to me? I could see me turning up at the yard to see to Drummer in that!

"There are some lovely shops in Fairview," Skinny rambled on, oblivious to my plans for her wheels. Of course, I realized, the red number would probably be long gone by the time I reached seventeen. Skinny would upgrade.

With a tiny main street and lots of cafés and boutiques, Fairview was as picturesque as it was expensive. Skinny sailed into a boutique called Madelaine, trying on boots and sweaters and jackets with prices that would keep Drummer in hay all winter. And she kept holding things up against me and pushing me into changing rooms to try them on.

So I did. Well, wouldn't you? I tried on an eye-wateringly expensive designer T-shirt that looked great and a pair of designer jeans that were too long, but who cares, and a pair of boots with heels I knew my mom would put her foot down about—and not in a good way. Skinny shook her head at the length of the jeans and told me I'd break my ankle in the boots (which was more than possible, regrettably), but she bought me the T-shirt without a second glance at the price, handing over the plastic and punching in her PIN. I almost fell over!

Then we went for a coffee, and I had a chocolate muffin and a Coke and Skinny had a latte, and thus fortified, we went onto another boutique called JayCee where Skinny was welcomed like a long-lost relative. When she spent a couple of hundred dollars in there on a blouse and a belt, I realized why. Yup, two hundred bucks on a blouse and a belt—and the belt was on sale!

Welcome to Skinny Lynny's world, I thought, hugging my T-shirt and feeling guilty for loving it so much. But then, I reasoned, actually my dad was paying, not Skinny, because although Skinny Lynny goes to work, my dad earns most of the money. And as Skinny pounded her PIN in again, my cell chimed with a text. Flipping it open, I saw it was from Bean.

ALL MESSED UP HERE AGAIN—CALL ME!

Oh. Oh pooh, I thought, my momentary shopping buzz oozing down to my toes. I dialed Bean's number, but her phone was off. I didn't dare leave a message in case she listened to it within earshot of anyone else, so I texted her instead: U CALL ME!

With Skinny's blouse and belt safely encased in a cool JayCee bag, we continued window-shopping along Fairview's main street—but my heart was no longer in shopping. I was far too worried about Bean's message. What could possibly have happened? Had Jazz been discovered? If so, how? Had her dad found her? Or, even more worryingly, could it be about Drummer? Had something happened? Tensely chewing the inside of my cheek, I tried to rekindle an interest in belts and boots and dresses with outrageous price tags without success.

"How's Drummer?" asked Skinny Lynny, flicking her hair back behind her ears and showing off a twinkly, dangly earring. It was as though she could see inside my head. Spooky! I remembered how, following me giving Skinny Lynny a riding lesson on Drum in the summer, she had taken up riding at a swanky riding school nearby, Stocks Farm. So I asked her how it was going.

"Oh, OK," she said airily. "I still go occasionally—it got more interesting when I started cantering and jumping, but it's not like I'm addicted to it. I mean, I like wearing all the clothes, and there's a lovely gray horse there called Cloud that I like, but it's not my favorite thing to do. I know you love it, Pia—and I know your dad got all excited about us going riding together, but this is fun, too, isn't it?"

I nodded because actually, before Bean's worrying text, it had been. It was a change to go shopping and be able to try on stuff that I normally couldn't afford. And—and this was the strange bit—Skinny was actually OK when she wasn't with my dad. She didn't grin and flirt and act all little-girly. She was much more, well, *ordinary* somehow. I felt a bit guilty for not disliking her as usual and wondered why I felt that way. I was just so used to her being the enemy. Mom and I had both blamed Skinny for enticing Dad away from us, but I was beginning to realize that Dad hadn't needed much in the way of enticement. He seemed really happy with Skinny. *More so than when he'd been with us*, I thought with a pang.

If only Bean would call me and I could get up to speed, I could have continued to enjoy shopping some more. However much I willed my cell to ring, it stayed stubbornly silent. I kept checking it to make sure I hadn't missed a call but no—nothing. Why *didn't* Bean call?

"Are you expecting a call from James?" asked Skinny, pausing to look at shoes in a shop window.

"No, my friend Bean. She's looking after Drummer," I explained, shoving my phone back in my bag.

"Oh, look at those gorgeous boots," Skinny cooed, drawing me into the shoe shop and trying on a pair of white boots adorned with fringe and studs. "Try those suede boots, Pia," she added. "They'll look great with your jeans."

She was right. I looked at the black suede toes peeping out from under the denim and wondered whether Skinny was going to buy them for me, too. I hoped so. They were just gorgeous. But why didn't Bean call?

I got the boots. I didn't even ask for them. Skinny just decided they were destined for my feet. I hoped Mom was going to be OK with it all—I didn't want to upset her, and I knew she could never afford the prices Skinny had paid for my new stuff. Target and Kohl's were our usual haunts. I felt really torn. Shopping with Skinny had almost been fun—and not just because she'd bought me stuff. It seemed the shopping trip had worked as a bonding exercise, after all. It could turn out to be a good day—if only Bean would call!

It all changed when we got back home and met up with Dad.

"Hi, Pumpkin!" he said, kissing both of us. "Did you have a good day?"

I nodded, showing him the designer T-shirt and boots. Frustration about Bean made me brave.

"Dad," I said carefully, "would you mind not calling me Pumpkin? I'm a bit old for that now."

"She is, Paul. Pia's a young lady now!" Skinny Lynny laughed, reverting back to her giggly and annoying persona around my dad. Actually, I was fed up with being Pumpkin. What was wrong with Pia? My name had been chosen by my mom and dad, for goodness sake, you'd think my dad would want to call me by it.

"OK then, if you think so," said Dad, ruffling my hair. One way or the other he was determined to keep me his little girl.

I kept checking my phone as Dad and Skinny discussed

where we could all go for dinner that evening before they took me back home. I was going to be home too late to go to the yard, which was annoying, but at least it meant I had all of Wednesday to be with Drummer and get up to speed with Bean.

Is there anything more frustrating than a cell phone that doesn't ring when you've been given only a fraction of the picture by text? If there is, I can't think what it can be! Finally, after some more totally unnecessary comments from Dad and Skinny about whether I was expecting a call from James (give it a rest, will you?), I took refuge in the putty-colored guest room and got ready to go out.

The weather had turned gloomy and rain pelted my window, making me think about Jazz. Huddled in the ice-house in the dark would be bad enough, but with the rain beating down, I could imagine how miserable it would be. Closing my eyes, I pictured Falling Snow sheltering next to a rhododendron bush, her head low, resting one hind leg, rainwater dripping off her sodden mane and tail. I imagined Jazz and her dog huddled together in the spooky ice-house on Drummer's exercise sheet, the door ajar so Jazz could make out her pony's outline in the gloom. *Brrrrr!* I was comfy in the bedroom with its en suite bathroom. The thought made me feel strangely guilty.

I pulled on my new T-shirt and grinned when I saw the designer label exposed between my shoulder blades. I'd have to tie my hair back to make sure that was on show! All the seams were sewn up to prevent them from fraying—a big change from the cheap shirts I usually wore. As I pulled my new left boot onto my foot, my phone rang AT LAST.

Snatching it off the bedside table, I slipped and toppled over onto the floor, banging my elbow on the polished floorboards. So not funny.

It was Bean—*finally!* "Bean," I practically shouted, "what's happening?"

"Hi, Pia, hold on a minute…" I couldn't believe it! I didn't want to hold on a minute, so I yelled into my phone, "Hey, Bean, talk to me NOW!" Rude, yes, but wouldn't you? There were lots of muffled shuffling sounds, then the sound of a stable door banging shut and Bean's voice again.

"Hello?"

"Bean, what are you doing? I'm dying for news here!" I shouted.

"Yeah, well, I'm in Tiff's stable, making sure no one can hear me," Bean mumbled indignantly. "Walls have ears, you know!"

"What's been happening?"

"Tons of stuff has happened. For a start, Jazz's father's been on the warpath," said Bean. I could tell she was whispering. "James and Cat saw him when they were out riding yesterday, and he ranted and raved at them, shouting that somebody had to know where his daughter and her pony were."

"I know that. Katy told me yesterday. I told you!"

"Oh, yes, I forgot. Anyway, now everybody knows Jazz

is missing. And then, as if that wasn't enough…oh, hold on a sec…"

Everything went quiet. What was Bean doing now? It was like torture, being given glimpses and then nothing again. Would I ever get to the bottom of things with Bean as my confidante? I wondered whether she could put Drummer on the phone, I'd get a more concise report from my pony than my friend! Maybe I should have asked Katy to help me after all…

"Hello, are you still there?" Bean's voice whispered out of my phone again.

"Yes, but where do you keep disappearing to?" I asked. Then I wished I hadn't.

"Well, Mrs. Bradley keeps walking past Tiff's stable—you know how she keeps forgetting things and makes about a zillion trips from Henry's stable to the tack room and back—she must get her riding boots resoled every few weeks—and Katy's around, too, and I don't want anyone to overhear me, for reasons which will become obvious (*When?* I thought!), and Dee's just come back from schooling Dolly. When I first dialed your number, the yard was deserted, but as soon as you answered, it seems the whole world and his wife, dog, cat, ferret, and bag of candy suddenly turned up. It's not easy being a spy!"

"Candy?" I asked.

"Huh?"

I closed my eyes and groaned. "Nothing, go on, tell me what else has happened!"

"What?"

"You said that wasn't all," I said slowly. I wanted to scream.

"What wasn't?"

"I don't know—you're telling me, remember?" I hissed.

"Er, oh, yes!" Bean took a deep breath. "James and Cat came back, and Cat was spitting nails, totally fed up with being shouted at by Jazz's dad, and she made a lot of noise about how she just knew you had something to do with Jazz's disappearance, you know, really stirring things up for you, so I had to be particularly spyish and look innocent. And then this morning, Jazz's dad turned up at the stable in his huge black 4x4 with a big dog inside, which threw itself at the car windows looking like it wanted to eat us all for lunch. And Jazz's dad banged on Mrs. Collins's front door, making Squish go ballistic, and he shouted that someone was hiding his daughter and they had better tell him where she was or there was going to be trouble, and he would see to it that whoever was helping her would wish they hadn't been born, as well as plenty of other unpleasant things, which I'm trying to put out of my mind."

"What did Mrs. C say?" I gulped, closing my eyes.

"She gave as good as she got! She may be bonkers, but you know she's as tough as old boots. She stood there in her slippers, shoved her fist in his face, and told him that no one at her yard knew anything, which was a lie, but she didn't know that, and that she was going to call the police if he didn't leave immediately."

"Then what?" I held my breath. How much worse could it possibly get?

"He went, but not until he'd stuck his face over most of the stable doors, saying he knew his pony was somewhere around, which freaked out all the ponies, not to mention Cat and Sophie, who added their protests at his behavior. Oh, and Bambi almost bit him, you know how she snakes her head about over her top door whenever anyone goes past her stable?" Bean added, taking a deep breath before continuing.

"But, hey, get this, Twiddles had climbed on the 4x4's hood, 'cause it was warm, which was another reason why the dog in the car had been in such a tizzy, especially as Twiddles just stared at it like it was crazy, which it probably was, and Twiddles had snuggled down for a nap, so when Jazz's dad had finished upsetting everyone and all the ponies, he tried to get him off. Only Twiddles puffed himself up and went for him, spitting in that charming way he does, scratching Jazz's father's hand and making him even more angry. He was red when he drove up the drive. You should have been here! It was *pandemonium!*"

I didn't think I'd ever be grateful for being at Dad's place, but I was so, so glad I *hadn't* been at the stable yard. It sounded like a complete nightmare.

"Mrs. C gave everyone the third degree, demanding that no one, but no one—she was very precise on that point—was to go near the traveler's camp or talk to them or anything, and we all had to promise we knew nothing about anything."

"What did you say?" I asked, holding my breath.

"Well, what could I say?" replied Bean. "I just nodded and kept my head down. Only Cat just had to stir it up for you. She said she was certain that you were best friends with the missing girl and bound to know something about it."

"What did Mrs. C say about that?" I asked, dreading the reply.

"Said she'd talk to you when you got back. But don't worry, she'll have forgotten about it by then, you know how vague she is."

Not if Cat keeps reminding her, I thought grimly.

"How is Jazz?" I asked faintly.

"Fine. Great. Tiff and I rode over there this afternoon with some more supplies—Tiff's getting used to the back-pack now. Jazz was a bit less suspicious of me today."

"Are you sure no one saw you?" I asked.

"Absolutely. Katy was in the school with James, and Cat had gone out riding by herself. Dee was grooming Dolly, and Leanne wasn't at the yard. I slipped out while they were all occupied. Stop worrying."

"Cat went riding alone?" I said. Why didn't that sound right?

"Yes. It was windy today, too. Oh, you know that old tree by the Winding Canter, the one at the top of the hill?"

"Yes," I said, my mind still confused and trying to grab hold of something I felt I'd missed, something I was sure was important.

"It's blown down. Right across the path. Makes a cool jump—only it took me half an hour to get Tiff anywhere near it because she was convinced it was going to eat her. You know what she's like."

I heard Dad shouting up the stairs.

"Anything else?" I asked, pulling myself up and sitting on the bed.

"Isn't that enough? There was something else…a juicy bit of gossip…now what was it…?"

What she had already told me was enough really, enough to make me wonder whether it really would be better if I stayed with Dad for a few more days. I never thought I'd ever consider that an attractive option. If anyone found out Bean and I had helped Jazz, I was in mega, mega trouble.

"How's Drummer?" I asked, hoping to get onto safer ground.

"Oh, well, that's another thing…" said Bean.

"What?" I screamed, jumping to my feet. "What's the matter? Tell me NOW!"

"Oh, Pia, lighten up!" Bean laughed. "Drummer's fine—and he's loving being on vacation with his Auntie Bean!"

I heard Skinny yelling up the stairs that she and Dad were ready to go. "Gotta go!" I told Bean. "See you tomorrow morning."

"Oh, wait a minute, I've remembered the other thing," said Bean. Gossip, I thought, relaxing. That might be some relief. "James broke up with Cat today."

How wrong could I be?

CHAPTER 14

I PEDALED TO THE YARD so fast on Wednesday morning, I thought I was going to have a heart attack. I could feel my heart thumping inside my chest, and my legs felt like jelly. That's the trouble with the yard being on top of a hill.

Drummer actually seemed pleased to see me.

"You're back!" he said, nuzzling my pockets for the treats he knew would be there. I offered him the fancy sugar lumps I'd swiped, and he crunched them down in seconds. "Is that all?" he asked, frisking me some more.

"You should have made them last longer," I told him, pulling his ears gently. I was so pleased to see him—it seemed like we'd been apart for weeks. "Sugar dissolves, you know," he said.

"Did you miss me?" I asked him. "I missed you!"

"Of course you did," Drummer said smugly.

"I, on the other hand, had a lovely rest. Are we going riding today?"

"You bet!" I told him. "Just as soon as Bean gets here."

Dee-Dee was already schooling Dolly, and Leanne had gone to a dressage show so Mr. Higgins's stable door was wide open, his new bed already laid for him for when they got back. I desperately didn't want to see James or

Cat—that would be too awkward. From the stalls on either side of Drummer, I could hear Moth munching on her hay, and I could see Bambi dozing with her head over her half door. She was deliberately ignoring Drum as usual.

I had Drum groomed and tacked up by the time Bean arrived on her bike.

"I'll be right there—I'll just brush the bits where the tack goes," she cried, disappearing into Tiffany's stable with her tack. I didn't like to point out that's what she always does.

Getting Tiffany ready in a rush is not recommended. Bean's palomino is such a nervous wreck, she hates to be hassled. When Bean led her out and mounted, Tiffany was in just the right mood to see ghosts and gremlins everywhere. It drives Drummer mad.

"Ahhh, what's that glistening thing?" I heard Tiffany exclaim, her head high, every muscle ready to flee as Bean threw her leg over the back of the saddle and fished about for her stirrup.

"It's a puddle of water." Drummer sighed, shaking his head.

"Oh, yes. I see that now," Tiffany said. "Hold on! Something's moving by the tree!"

"Yes, a wisp of hay," Drummer said slowly. "Now get a grip and let's go!"

We were going to see Jazz, of course.

I'd smuggled out some apples, oranges, a banana, half a loaf of bread, some cheese, some chips, a whole load of granola bars, and some chocolate. I'd also liberated some canned ham we'd had in the cupboard for years, with one of those keys on the side you use to break into it. It was part of Mom's just-in-case supplies, whatever that meant.

I had all the provisions in my bulging backpack, and as we rode off down the drive, Cat's dad drove past, his daughter sitting in his passenger seat beside him. Bean rode up beside me to hide the backpack from view. Close!

"I bet Cat's upset about James," Bean said. "She's liked him forever, and he was quite a catch. Everyone at school was talking about them going out together."

"She doesn't look upset," I replied. Cat had looked out of the window and smirked at me as her father drove past. Usually she ignored me. I wondered what was going on. "What happened?" I asked Bean.

"James dumped her," she said bluntly.

"But do you know why?"

"Nope! But I bet the story varies, depending on who you ask."

I couldn't get too elated about James and Cat no longer being an item right now. I had other bigger and scarier issues. Namely, Jazz's dad! I'd save the celebrations until later. The image of Cat smirking at me was puzzling.

"Come on," said Bean, shortening her reins and sitting a nasty side step from Tiffany as she swerved around a discarded stroller. "Let's get going."

We rode to the icehouse by an indirect route, approaching from the other side of the lake, just in case we bumped into anyone. Drummer was on his toes and took all my attention, as I so didn't want to get bucked off in the mud. We found Jazz running her fingers through Falling Snow's mane, removing burrs clinging to the black and silver rainfall of horsehair cascading down her neck. Three pairs of eyes greeted us—the striking violet ones of Jazz, the suspicious amber eyes of her dog, and the dark, melting chocolate brown of Falling Snow's.

"Hello, Jazz," I said, sliding off Drummer and unfastening my backpack, letting it fall to the ground.

"You're back," Jazz replied, giving a meaningful glance toward Bean.

"I couldn't get here," I explained, shrugging my shoulders. "I had to think of something. You can trust Bean, you know that now."

Jazz nodded reluctantly.

Falling Snow had eaten most of the grass in the clearing, and now she stood in mud. I could see the door to the icehouse was open, nothing inside but uninviting darkness. How could Jazz spend the night here, I wondered. On the plus side, Jazz's dog seemed to have given up growling at me. He lay with his front paws stretched out in front of him, his eyes never straying from us and the ponies.

"Are you all right?" I asked.

Jazz nodded. "Perfectly. Has my dad gone yet?"

"No, he's been threatening everyone instead," Bean told her.

"Apparently, your father has been searching for you," I

told Jazz, "and not in a very friendly way. I don't think he's just going to up and leave. He must be worried about you."

"Worried he's lost Falling Snow, you mean!" retorted Jazz. Her change of mood prompted the dog to rise to his feet, a growl growing in the back of his throat. Tiffany took a step backward and rolled her eyes. Drummer stood his ground and stared back at the dog.

"Well, whatever, but he's been to our yard making threats and scaring people. I'm not surprised you ran away from him. He's really scary!" retorted Bean.

"That is the *Armaya* working," said Jazz matter-of-factly. "I'm never going back," she insisted, her violet eyes sparkling. "He won't stay forever. He'll think I've gone, and he'll leave eventually."

"How long do you think you can stay here?" I asked, looking at the muddy ground under the ponies' hooves. "There isn't enough grass here for Falling Snow."

"I know that," Jazz said. "She's already lost weight."

I turned to the dark gray pony and could see she looked a little thinner. The nights had been cold recently, and she needed hay to keep warm.

"I'm all right," Falling Snow told me. "I feel fine. Tell her I'm all right."

"You need more food than there is here," Drummer said.

"Have you got nothing else to eat but the grass?" Tiffany asked, aghast. "But there's nothing here!"

"Falling Snow says she's all right," I told Jazz.

"Well, we both know that she isn't," Jazz replied.

"I know. I'll bring you some pony cubes this afternoon. She really needs hay, but I can't very well bring a bale of that."

"We can bring a hay net each," suggested Bean. "We can carry them on our backs. I'm sure the ponies won't mind."

Mmmm, I thought. Drummer won't, but Tiffany will probably think a tiger was hitching a ride. Perhaps Drummer could talk her into it, if I couldn't.

"You're good friends," Jazz said. "I didn't think I could be friends with anyone *gadjikane*, but you've proved me wrong."

"Well, actually," began Bean, wading in, all tact abandoned, "everyone at the yard thinks your group is hard on their horses, and some are convinced you'll steal stuff. It was only Pia who thought differently."

I winced, but Jazz didn't seem to be offended. "I think my father and his friends are hard on their horses, too. But we treasure them. Horses are our history, our lives, and our currency. House dwellers will never understand that."

"One of the horses at the yard used to belong to travelers," continued Bean, unable to stop herself now she had started. "She was badly treated, and James rescued her."

"But she was badly treated by the boys from the factory—Moth couldn't get away because she was tethered. We don't like to see horses tethered," I explained.

"The chestnut mare with the white face—that's who you mean, isn't it?" said Jazz.

I nodded. "How did you know?"

"I felt it."

A shiver ran up and down my spine as I remembered

how Jazz had stroked Moth and how the chestnut pony had reacted. I had never seen her act in such a positive way with anyone, not even James.

"We have no choice but to tether our horses," Jazz continued.

"Yes, but Moth was tied up quite a distance from the travelers' camp," said Bean, determined to tell Jazz the full story. "So no one knew when the boys were treating Moth badly. That's the problem—you just tie them up and leave them—anyone could steal them, ill-treat them, or anything!"

"Finding grazing is sometimes difficult," Jazz said sullenly. "You'd be just as upset if we left our horses tethered on mud. According to you, we can't do anything right."

The atmosphere in the clearing was suddenly tense. It was time to go.

"We'll be back later with food for Falling Snow," I said, emptying my backpack and mounting Drummer. "She's the one on mud at the moment."

As Jazz stepped back, Drum took a step toward her as though attached by a thread. Only my hand on the rein restrained him.

I felt a clutch at my heart, and in an instant, something I had always failed to grasp clicked into place. I had struggled to understand how I had made such an easy enemy when I had first arrived at Laurel Farm, but as Jazz held my pony's attention in a way I never could, everything became startlingly clear. As my jealousy of Jazz's unique affinity with horses and ponies hit me, I imagined how things would be if Jazz kept Falling Snow at Laurel Farm; how it would be if she had an unexplained empathy with the ponies. The way I would feel if that was to happen hit me like a thunderbolt and with absolute certainty.

I wouldn't like it. I wouldn't like it at all.

Cat had been the one everyone had turned to for advice before I'd arrived, and Epona had given me the ability to hear and talk to the ponies. For the first time I fully appreciated how Cat felt about me.

No wonder she hated me.

Chapter 15

My archrival was picking out Bambi's hooves in the yard when Bean and I rode back along the drive. Bambi was wearing her saddle, and her legs were muddy. It appeared that Cat had been out for a ride, too.

"Uh-oh," I hissed to Bean. "Cat alert!"

Wriggling out of my backpack, I steered Drum over to one side of the drive and threw it in to the bushes. No need to arouse suspicion.

Cat scowled at me, and Bambi put her ears back at Drummer as we halted outside Drum's stable. Drummer couldn't help himself...

"You're looking good today, Bambi," he murmured.

"Go pull a cart!" Bambi replied, swishing her tail.

"I'd rather pull you!" said Drummer, sighing. Talk about corny. If that was my pony's best pickup line, then no wonder Bambi wasn't interested.

Cat leaned on her pony's skewbald back, body brush in one hand, currycomb in the other. "Will you ever stop annoying my pony, Mia?" she asked, a sour look that matched Bambi's crossing her face.

"Bambi's always making faces at Drummer," I replied, "you know that. She likes doing it. Just like you do."

"I know about you and that traveler girl," Cat said, her green eyes shining.

"You're delusional," I said, trying to be aloof.

"I can't believe you'd put all our ponies in danger for the sake of that lowlife."

She knew nothing about Jazz, and yet she was calling her names.

"There's no need to take it out on everyone else, you know," I said sweetly. "It isn't Jazz's fault you're not going out with James anymore." I knew it was nasty, but she had totally asked for it.

Surprisingly, the smirk returned. It wasn't what I'd expected.

"You think you're so clever," Cat said. "You won't be soon."

"I don't know what you're talking about," I said in what I hoped was a casual and innocent manner. My heart was beating faster. There was no way Cat could know anything, but I still felt guilty. I prayed it didn't show on my face.

"You won't feel so smart when they're gone," Cat went on. "I bet you anything you want that they won't leave empty-handed."

"Oh, are the travelers going?" I said, running up Drummer's stirrups. "It sounds like you know more about them than I do. Perhaps *you're* the one who's helping Jazz."

"We both know who's helping her," snapped Cat.

"You're talking nonsense," I replied, leading Drummer into his stable, turning him round, and closing the stable door.

"That told her!" said Drummer, snatching at his hay net

and taking a great mouthful of hay, which he couldn't eat because he was still wearing his bridle.

"What time do you want to go back to Jazz this afternoon?" Bean whispered as I hung Drum's bridle in the tack room, wiping bits of gunky hay off his bit.

"Er, about two o'clock?" I suggested.

"Fine. I'll get the pony cubes ready, and as soon as the coast is clear, I'll hide a couple of hay nets at the end of the drive. I don't think mounting up in the yard and riding off with a hay net bouncing about on each of our backs would go unnoticed."

"Mmmm, good plan," I agreed.

Bean went outside to watch Dee and Katy schooling. Moth was out in the field—James was obviously busy doing other things—and probably avoiding Cat. With a couple of hours to spare, I thought I might as well do something useful, so I got on with a job I'd been meaning to do for a while—clear out Drummer's tack box. Tipping everything out onto the yard outside the tack room, I sorted through it and divided it into two piles; one pile full of things that I wanted to keep, the other into stuff I didn't.

How does so much junk accumulate in tack boxes? I hauled out used baby wipes, tissues, old chip bags, a very moldy something that I thought might once have been a carrot, a couple of lids from cans of things long used up, a lead rope clip that I had thought might come in handy and hadn't, several hair scrunchies, a white ribbon I hadn't been too impressed with (which didn't look very white now), a show schedule from a year ago, a broken cell phone charm of a pony that looked like Drum, and two pens. The bottom of the tack box was awash with spilled hoof oil, so I added a soaked sponge to the pile of trash. Then I boiled a kettle, took some of the dish-washing soap that was next to it, and sat on the bench outside the tack room scrubbing the tack box inside and out.

From the bench I caught occasional glimpses of Drum as he walked around his stable and munched on his hay, and then noticed Cat bridling Bambi again. *That is weird*, I thought. Was she going riding again? It was a strange and strained atmosphere with only us on the yard, but I was determined not to be intimidated by Cat. I didn't want her to think she had me on the run.

Squish came over and settled down beside me with a grunt, watching the sparrows swooping down from the tree by Moth's stable, searching for fallen feed from the ponies' buckets. When the sun came out, it felt warm on my face, despite the autumn chill in the air.

Hearing car wheels on the gravel drive, I turned, expecting to see a familiar car—Mrs. Bradley's perhaps, or the farrier's van or the postman for Mrs. Collins. I didn't recognize the small blue hatchback that rolled past and parked next to Mrs. Collins's beater.

I glanced across the yard. Cat seemed tense. What was going on?

The car's inhabitants—a woman with two young girls—clattered into the yard. One girl looked about six,

the other was in the woman's arms, clearly only a toddler. The older one wore pink trousers, a pale blue quilted
jacket, and a riding helmet, and she ran up to Cat, squealing
with delight.

"Shhhh," said Cat, her voice kind. Bending down, she
swung the young girl up in her arms. "You must always
talk quietly and move slowly around horses because although they're big, they're nervous. There, you can stroke
her now, she won't hurt you."

The girl patted Bambi's forehead, and the mare nuzzled
the girl, making her giggle.

The woman looked familiar, but I couldn't remember
where I had seen her before. Perhaps she just had one of
those faces.

I rinsed out the tack box and turned it upside down to
drain. Then I fetched Drummer's bridle and started cleaning that, too. My mind kept working. Where had I seen
the woman—and her two children? I was certain all three
were locked in my memory banks somewhere.

I watched as Cat untied Bambi and tightened her girth.
Then she pulled down the stirrups and lifted the girl up
onto her pony's back.

I had seen them before. And the girl had ridden Bambi
then. It was at one of the Sublime Equine Challenge
shows. That was it! The woman had lifted the girl onto
Bambi's back, and Cat had looked very unhappy about
it but had said nothing. It had been very odd. And now
they were all here, and the girl was riding Bambi again.

And Cat looked no happier about it this time. What was going on?

Between shortening the girl's stirrups and showing her how to hold the reins, Cat completely ignored me. I tried to pretend I wasn't interested, but I was. Very. It was all coming back to me. The last time the woman and the children had appeared, Katy and Bean had gone all mysterious, like there was some big secret going on that they had sworn never to tell. And Cat had been upset enough afterward to try to get me eliminated from the Sublime Equine Challenge. So what were the woman and her kids doing here at the yard, playing riding school?

Would anyone tell me the secret now?

With the woman and toddler trailing along behind, Cat led Bambi along the drive, causing Drummer to lean over his door and neigh to Bambi's disappearing backside like she was the last pony in the world, even though Tiffany was in her stable opposite.

"Hey!" I yelled. "I'm here!"

"Oh, big deal. Why can't I go out in the field?"

"We're going riding again this afternoon. You know that."

"Well, I could go out for an hour or so, you know, chill out."

"You'll roll and get all muddy."

"You can put a turnout rug on me."

"No. Sorry."

"Is it Christmas already?"

"No, why?"

"I thought I saw you cleaning my bridle."

"Oh, very funny!"

"You wouldn't think so if you had to wear it."

With the bit gleaming and the leatherwork clean and supple, I returned Drummer's bridle to the tack room and started on his saddle. *I have to schedule more time for tack cleaning*, I thought, *Drummer's saddle is a disgrace!* I had almost finished when Katy, Dee, and Bean returned from the school.

"Oooooo, Pia, you can clean Bluey's tack if you like!" Katy said hopefully.

"Get lost!" I snorted. "I'll watch you clean it instead."

"Yoo-hoo, Drummer!" I heard Dolly shout across the yard. Drum glanced out over his stable door before ducking back inside again. He thinks Dolly's a man-eater.

"We're riding to the Quickmart to get some chocolate. Want anything, Pia?" asked Katy.

"Can you get me some licorice?" I said, fishing about in my pocket for some coins. "Cat's got visitors," I added.

"Oh, yes?" Bean sniffed and fished about in her pockets for a Kleenex.

"A woman with two young children. The same woman who was at the Sublime Equine Challenge."

Unable to find a tissue, Bean wiped her nose on the back of her hand. "Gross," she said sheepishly, "but totally better than *not* wiping it!"

I ignored her. "The woman," I continued, "who is she? One of the kids is riding Bambi."

Bean shrugged her shoulders and stared down the drive. "How should I know?" she said. "Hold on, I'm coming, too!" she yelled, grabbing her bike and pedaling after Bluey's and Dolly's backsides.

It was obvious she still didn't want to tell me anything. It was so frustrating!

When Bambi returned, the woman and her kids didn't hang about. As soon as the blue car had disappeared out of the yard, Cat hastily altered her stirrups, grabbed her riding helmet, and, mounting Bambi, rode off along the bridle path in a hurry.

I had other things to worry about. Two o'clock came quickly and, picking a moment when Dee and Katy were occupied, Bean and I saddled the ponies, filled the retrieved backpack full of pony cubes, dug out the hay nets from the hedge, and headed for the lake in a roundabout route, the hay nets bouncing about on our backs.

"Nasty growth you've got there!" giggled Bean as Tiffany put in another spurt. Out of the corner of her eye, the palomino could catch glimpses of the hay net bouncing about, causing her to shy and dart about.

"You look like the hunchback of Notre Dame," I replied. Drummer couldn't care less about the hay net on my back. He thought it was a packed lunch. I hoped he wouldn't kick up when he found out it wasn't for him.

As we drew close to the icehouse we fell silent, glancing around behind us to make sure we weren't being followed. Halting, we listened. Nothing. No hoofbeats, no clink of a bit, only the rustling of the trees and unconcerned bird-song. I hoped Jazz wasn't still upset with us after our tethering disagreement.

We pushed our way into the clearing, the branches springing back behind us like doors in a Western saloon, hiding us from the rest of the world.

The clearing was empty. No Jazz, no scary dog, no Falling Snow.

"Oh," I heard someone say. It was me. The door to the icehouse stood open, and I could see Drummer's exercise rug on the floor with all the food we had brought Jazz that morning. A bottle of water lay on its side, its contents half leaked on the grass, and the muddy ground was full of footprints, evidence of visitors.

"Where are they?" asked Bean. I looked around. On the opposite side of the clearing

I could see a gap in the bushes. Someone had forced their way in…and forced Jazz, Kasali, and Falling Snow out.

CHAPTER 16

"THAT'S THAT, THEN." BEAN sighed as we rode home side by side. The ponies were silent, locked in their own thoughts about Falling Snow and Jazz having been discovered by her father. It had to be him. But how had he known where to look? It wasn't like you could get a vehicle through the woods, and the icehouse was fantastically well concealed. Had her father just stumbled upon it by luck?

However it had happened, Jazz's plans had come to an abrupt end. I didn't see how Jazz could escape again. Even if she did, where could she go?

"Do you think her father really will sell Falling Snow?" asked Bean.

I shrugged my shoulders, not trusting myself to speak.

"I'm sorry I was so horrible about Jazz to begin with, Pia," Bean continued. "You were right; she loves Falling Snow just as much as we love Tiffany and Drummer—although that dog of hers gives me the creeps. I can't imagine how I would feel if my dad told me he was selling Tiffany. And Falling Snow is so gentle. It makes me cry just thinking about her being forced to race. It's not Jazz's fault her father's so mean and the others race their horses so hard."

I shut my eyes tight. I couldn't bear to think about it. About Falling Snow being raced again, being sold to the highest bidder, to run and run until she broke down. And what would Jazz do then?

"You don't suppose Jazz will tell her dad about us, do you?" said Bean.

I hoped not. "I'm sure she won't," I said firmly. "Why would she?"

"I don't know," said Bean. "But if they beat their horses when they race, they might beat Jazz, too. She might be *forced* to tell him."

I shivered. What a can of worms that would open! I imagined Jazz's dad lying in wait for me at the end of the yard drive, imagined a huge man with black eyes, wild hair, and an unreasonable disposition, bearing down on me and cursing me and future generations of my family. I wished— for the umpteenth time—that I had no imagination.

Leaning forward, I patted Drummer's fluffy bay neck to give myself courage. I still hadn't got around to booking him in to be clipped, what with the Jazz and Falling Snow drama and having had to stay with Dad. I couldn't get my head around that now, not with Jazz recaptured and Falling Snow's future in jeopardy. My brain felt like a heaped up plate of spaghetti again, all tangled and impossible to make sense of.

We rode back into the yard as night fell, the lights from the stables warm and inviting. I put Drum's tack away then made my way to the barn. With a heavy heart I turned Drummer's soggy exercise rug inside out to dry off. Black-and-white hairs were mixed with Drummer's red ones. The rug hadn't kept Jazz dry in the icehouse after all; Jazz had put it on her beloved pony to keep off the worst of the rain.

I felt like crying. Poor Jazz, she loved Falling Snow so much and now all her efforts and scheming and determination were for nothing. It wasn't fair! What was happening to her now, I wondered. Was she tied up in a trailer? Or nursing bruises? Or sobbing in a corner as her father put plans in motion to sell her pony? Maybe Falling Snow had already been promised to someone else and had, even now, changed owners.

"You're back then, Tia. Where have you been, as if I didn't know!" *Oh, great*, I thought as Cat walked into the barn. She was her usual buoyant, cocky self.

I was so not in the mood for this. Instead of ignoring her, I snapped.

"Who's the mystery woman with the two kids?" I asked.

For just a second, I saw a flicker of doubt replace Cat's usual expression, but then the sneer was back.

"That's none of your business, nosy!" she snapped.

"OK, if you don't feel like telling me, I'll just ask Bambi," I said with an exaggerated smile, realizing that was quite a good idea. I didn't usually strike up a conversation with Cat's skewbald mare, for obvious reasons, but maybe I could get around her and ease some info out of her with a few carrots or mints. *Ding!* went my brain like the oven timer. Why didn't I think of that before?

I decided not to hang around and enjoy the look of fury on Cat's face. Brushing past her, I went back to settle

Drummer for the night, my thoughts returning to Jazz and Falling Snow. How had it all gone so wrong? *But then*, I thought, *Jazz probably never stood a chance of escaping with her pony.* It had just been a desperate attempt to ward off the inevitable—her pony being sold. Putting my arm on Drummer's neck, I tried to imagine how I would feel in that position. Sensing my mood, Drummer nuzzled me.

"It's all gone wrong, hasn't it?" he said.

I nodded, feeling choked.

"Well, you did your best."

"It wasn't enough," I replied, sniffing.

"There wasn't much more you could have done, and you at least gave Jazz your support," Drum told me. "You were there when she needed a friend. That must have meant a lot to her."

I leaned on Drummer's solid bay neck, feeling his warmth on the cold night. He always knows what to say to cheer me up when I'm feeling down. He's annoying, and he drives me crazy sometimes, but when the chips are down and I'm in need of a friend, he does it for me every time. He really is the best.

"Thanks for trying to cheer me up," I whispered.

"Now run along and get me a tea snack," he said. "It's late, and I'm hungry."

I knew his sympathy wouldn't last! I filled Drummer's hay net and mixed his feed. Then I tidied his bed and added some more bedding to make sure he was comfortable. Seeing to my pony's needs made me feel better, and flicking off the light, I settled myself in a corner so I could watch him eat. I love doing that when Drummer's in at nights. I can hear him munching and watch him doing what he loves best—eating—and it feels all warm and cozy as the light fades. Bean put her head over Drummer's half door.

"You all right?" she asked, sighing.

"Sort of," I replied.

"I've got to go," said Bean. "See you tomorrow?"

"Yup, see you."

I heard her bike creaking as she pedaled down the drive. I heard her shout good night to Mrs. Collins, heard Mrs. C call Squish and then slam her front door, heard Cat check Bambi's bolts and give her pony a carrot before running across the yard as her mom came to collect her, and then the yard was quiet, save for the usual rustling and munching of the horses and ponies in their stables. It was almost dark, but I could make out Drummer's shape as he shifted his weight from one back leg to the other, locking his leg into position so he could stand up without effort.

I sat hugging my knees, feeling the cold seep around me. I didn't want to go home yet. I just wanted to be still and quiet with Drummer and think about Jazz. What would happen to her? Poor Jazz. Poor Falling Snow. But there was nothing I could do. Nothing.

Suddenly, I heard a car crunch its way along the gravel drive. The car stopped, and the door slammed. Footsteps passed Drummer's door, and he stopped eating for a moment. Then he started chewing rhythmically again as I heard the click of a switch and saw light spilling out into the yard, filling up the black square that was Drum's open top door. The light was from Moth's stable—James had come to feed and water his pony. Either his mom or his dad—or possibly both—were still in the car. I could hear the muffled music of the car radio.

Shrinking back into the corner, I prayed James wouldn't look over Drummer's door. I didn't want to talk to James right now. I didn't know what to say to him; he had been understandably anti the travelers and Jazz, and I didn't know whether I was supposed to know about him and Cat breaking up. I didn't want to get Bean into trouble.

James's footsteps retreated, and then got louder as he walked from Moth's stable to the barn. I heard the tap running as he filled her water bucket, heard Moth's soft whinny as she watched him approaching with her feed, listened to James talking quietly to his chestnut mare, straightening her rug and checking her over.

"How're you doin', Moth?" he whispered. "Go over, now, let me straighten your bed. Good girl…"

Drummer shot me a quizzical look, but I shook my head. Sighing, he returned to his hay net, twirling it as he selected the best pieces of hay. It would take me ages to unravel it again in the morning.

I heard James's footsteps again. Then they stopped outside Drummer's stable. Obligingly, Drummer shoved his head over his door, blocking me from view.

"Hey there, Drummer," said James, patting Drum's bay head. Drummer blew gently through his nostrils. "I know you're in there, Pia," said James. I held my breath. He couldn't possibly know. "Your bike's leaning against the tack room." I groaned. How stupid was I? Knowing the game was up, Drummer backed up and returned to his hay net, exposing my terrible hiding place. James ran his hand through his hair and grinned. "Are you hiding?" he asked.

"Er, no, not really," I lied. "I'm just enjoying some quality time with Drum."

Drummer snorted. I ignored him.

"How were things at your dad's?" James asked.

"OK. How were things here?" I'd said it before I could stop myself. Honestly, how could I be so dense?

"Well, funny you should ask," began James. "Can I come in?"

"Er, OK," I said.

"What is this?" asked Drummer "My stable's not the YMCA, you know."

James joined me in the straw.

"Too many legs cluttering up the place, lounging about, getting in the way," grumbled Drummer. "Don't blame me if I stand on one or two of them."

"Watch out for Drum," I said. One person could comfortably curl up in a corner. Two people made the floor space a bit crowded, and I knew that if any grown-ups were around, they'd warn us about it being danger-ous. As Drummer walked over to his water bucket and took a long slurp, James tucked his knees up under his chin like me.

"I suppose you know that I broke up with Cat?" he said.

"Oh?" I lifted my eyebrows in feigned ignorance.

"Yes, thought it best. Things weren't exactly peachy between us."

"I thought you liked her," I said, blatantly fishing for info.

"Yeah, yeah, she's nice enough," James replied. "I just don't want to go out with her."

"Oh. I see," I said.

Lifting his head from the water bucket, Drummer spun around to his hay net, dribbling water from his mouth over our knees.

"Look out, Drum!" I cried.

"No, you look out," mumbled Drummer, dribbling even more.

"To tell you the truth," James continued, staring hard at his wet knees. "I only asked her out in the first place to stop her objecting about you in the Team Challenge at Brookdale and getting our whole team eliminated. Desperate measures and all that! You must have realized that."

"Er, well…"

"It wasn't very nice of me, was it? Not chivalrous. I'm not proud of it. Don't tell her, will you? She must never know."

"No, no, of course not," I said, shaking my head furiously, my heart soaring inside—James hadn't asked Cat out because he liked her. He'd asked her out to protect the team. Phew! I wondered if Cat had guessed the truth.

I would have wondered about it if I were Cat, but then, I'm paranoid.

"Want to go riding sometime?" asked James.

My heart took off like a rocket launcher.

"We haven't been riding together for ages," he went on.

"OK," I said, nodding, trying to play it a bit cool. I thought James would still be mad at me about standing up for Jazz, but he seemed to have forgotten about it.

"Did you hear about our nasty run-in with one of the travelers?" he asked.

I held my breath and nodded, not trusting myself to speak.

"Seems his daughter's run away. I'm not surprised. The guy's a total psycho!"

"So I heard," I mumbled.

"Good for her," continued James, with feeling. "She must be brave to run off with her pony. But then—" He turned and looked at me. I was glad it was dark, so he couldn't see my face. I wouldn't have been surprised if it had *yes, I know, I helped her* written all over it. "You always stood up for her, didn't you, Pia?"

"Er—well—um—" I stammered. "I wouldn't say I stood up for her, exactly." Was this where our riding date got nixed?

"He said *someone* was helping her…"

Oh, no. I could almost hear James's brain working. *Click, grind, ching…bingo!*

"Is it you? Only Bean's been acting strange lately, so I wondered whether it was her."

I wanted to deny it, but I thought it only fair to divert attention away from Bean and fess up. After all, I wasn't helping Jazz anymore. No one was. If James hated me afterward, well, then I'd have to deal with it. I took a deep breath.

"Sort of," I said slowly.

I felt James sit up. "How?" he whispered. He didn't sound angry, just curious.

"I showed her the old icehouse. She hid there with her pony and her dog."

James let out a low whistle, causing Drummer to stop chewing for a millisecond and flick his ears back toward the sound. "Wow, she's brave," James said. "That's not somewhere I'd choose to spend the night."

"So you understand why she had to run away?" I said, relieved to talk about it. "Her father was going to sell her pony. She ran away to save Falling Snow. I had to help her—I'd want someone to help me if Drummer was under threat. I didn't think anyone would ever find her at the icehouse. Practically no one knows about it, only us here at Laurel Farm. I mean, her father must have been lucky to have stumbled across it."

"What? He found her there?" asked James.

I realized that only Bean and I knew Jazz had been found. Until now, James thought she was still missing.

"I went back there today, and she was gone," I said, leaving out the fact that Bean had been with me. "She wouldn't have left there willingly—her father must have found her."

"She was at the icehouse…" James repeated to himself.

"Yes, I told you…"

"Her father wasn't lucky," James said slowly. "He knew where to look."

"No way!" I said, shaking my head. "How could he possibly know?"

"Because somebody told him," James replied grimly. All I could hear was my heart thudding. James's bombshell had done the impossible—Drummer had stopped chewing. But there was more. "And I know who it was!"

CHAPTER 17

MOM NOTICED I WASN'T MYSELF.

"What's up, honey?" she said, her face still red from her exertions at the gym as she flopped down on the sofa and took a swig from her water bottle. I don't know how she knew. I'd only said hello, so I must have looked morose. James's revelation was racing around my brain. I decided not to blab it this time.

"Mom, what would you do if you knew that a person had done something to hurt someone just because they hated them, just because they were different, even though they didn't really know them?"

"Anyone I know?" asked Mom.

I shook my head. "Not really."

"Goodness, I'm glad I'm not your age anymore." Mom sighed, rubbing her nose. "All that angst and trouble with relationships. I can remember it being exhausting!"

"Oh, right! Not like agonizing over boyfriends!" I exclaimed before I could stop myself.

Mom didn't get cross. She stopped in mid swig and lowered the water bottle. "You're right!" she said, her eyes wide. "It never stops, does it? When am I going to grow up?"

"Any ideas?" I asked, aware that the conversation had shifted from my problem to hers.

"Well, no. I mean, " Mom began, frowning, "I don't know when I'll grow out of this stage...and to be honest, Jerry..."

"No, Mom, any ideas about my dilemma?" Honestly, my mom got distracted so easily these days!

"Oh. Well, I'm not sure what you're asking me."

I thought for a bit. "No, I'm not sure either," I said. "I mean, should I confront the person who has been mean? Should I have it out with them?"

"Pia, I don't want you getting into any fights," said Mom.

That is good, I thought, *because that is the last thing I want, too.* So what did I want?

"Most people do horrible things because they're un-happy about something else," said Mom. "Or scared. You usually find they get what's coming to them. I mean, some-thing will happen to them as a sort of penance. It's karma."

I sighed. Karma again. I was getting totally fed up with karma popping up all the time. I heartily wished karma would take a hike. But it seemed I'd wandered onto dan-gerous ground.

"Of course, it sometimes takes a heck of a long time," continued Mom, her voice changing into her bitter-and-twisted mode that I hadn't heard for a while. "I'm still wait-ing for karma to catch up with little Miss Fluffy Brain!"

Uh-oh, I thought. Mom was referring to Skinny Lynny. *Her brain couldn't be that fluffy*, I thought. She'd managed to plan Dad's defection with military precision. Mom had raised her eyebrows when I'd showed her my new T-shirt and boots and asked me whether I'd had a nice time at my father's, to which I'd just nodded and shrugged a bit, so she didn't think I'd been whooping it up without her. Honestly, trying to be fair to both divorced parents was a job and a half. I was determined to show loyalty to Mom, mainly because she was on her own, and now I'd triggered a relapse. This time, however, Mom pulled herself out of it in record time.

"Things will work out, Pia," she concluded, anxious to move on. "Phew, I really gave that cross trainer a hammering tonight. I'm starving! Are you? Want a baked potato and salad?"

I was, but I didn't. I wanted takeout Chinese, but that wasn't going to happen. Should I take Mom's advice? What good would it do to confront Jazz's betrayer now? Nothing, I decided. What was done was done. But in the back of my mind was the nagging feeling that I was just wimping out. Was I just being cowardly?

The next day, I got to the yard early, to the surprise of Mrs. Collins who was feeding the cats in her pajamas—so not a pretty sight—and I hastily saddled Drummer.

"What's the hurry?" asked Drum, giving me an Oscar-worthy demonstration of theatrical yawning.

I'd been awake half the night, worrying about Jazz. "I have to see whether Falling Snow is still at the traveler camp," I said, dreading that Jazz's pony had already been sold. "I have to know what has happened to Jazz."

"Well, all right," replied Drummer, stretching one hind

leg out behind him and arching his neck. "But for good-ness sake, let's take it easy for the first ten minutes. It's a bit early for me. I'm not really a morning pony."

We walked down the gravel drive and along the bridle path. The weather had picked up, and the sun was trying to shine through small clouds that did their best to scuttle along in front of it and block its path. Rabbits, not used to early riders, were out grazing and bunny-hopping along the side of the fields, and we even spotted a couple of deer, which woke Drummer up. He swapped yawning for snort-ing, his head up, his tail lifted high, telling me he was ready if a deer came too close. But, of course, they didn't. They disappeared silently into the woods like ghosts.

Reaching the top of the hill, we both looked down onto the Sloping Field. My heart was thumping in my chest, and I could tell that Drummer was anxious, too. The travelers' trailers were dotted about, and there was plenty of activity in the camp. Children were pulling apart a stroller, a woman was sitting on the steps to her trailer, smoking, and several men stood around talking. A chained dog howled.

"Can you see her?" I asked Drum, my hand clutching his black mane for comfort.

Together we counted the tethered horses.

"Two piebalds, a chestnut, a gray…" My eyes darted from horse to horse, unwilling to acknowledge that an iron gray with white flecks on her coat was nowhere to be seen.

"I can't see her!" I wailed, despair washing over me. Jazz's father couldn't have sold her already! But there was no mistake; there was no Falling Snow.

"Perhaps Jazz has run away again?" Drum asked hopefully.

My heart soared. Could Drummer be right? Had Jazz fled again?

The howling intensified. Someone threw a piece of wood at the dog, chained to one of the 4x4s. It didn't stop. Narrowing my eyes and gazing closer, I suddenly gasped.

"That's Jazz's dog!"

"Oh," said Drummer.

"She's left her dog behind," I said. And then my heart sank as I realized the implication of the desolate dog tied to the car.

"She wouldn't leave Kasali, would she?" I whispered to Drum.

Drummer snorted. "No," he murmured. "I don't think she would."

So Jazz hadn't run away again. But Falling Snow was gone. I felt tears welling up behind my eyes. It was what Jazz had most feared. Her beloved Falling Snow had been sold. Her dog was chained—surely she must be held a prisoner, too. It had all been for nothing.

"I hoped you would come."

Drummer and I both jumped at the voice that seemed to come from nowhere. Drummer did a one-eighty turn in a single movement, which caused me to lurch onto his neck and clutch his mane in order to avoid hitting the ground.

"Jazz!" I cried, thrilled to see her.

"Falling Snow!" exclaimed Drummer.

"Why are you hanging around?" I said, before lowering my voice and glancing back at the Sloping Field. "You need to get away before your father discovers you."

Jazz laughed. "No, no, you've got it all wrong. I'm just out for a ride," she said. She wore her emerald green sweater and frayed jeans as usual, but her eyes were bright and she looked happy.

"We thought Falling Snow had been sold," I said.

"What about the dog?" Drummer said.

"Then we thought you'd managed to get away again," I explained.

"What about the dog?" Drummer said, louder this time.

Jazz shook her head and laughed. I didn't understand; I'd been wracked with images of Jazz beaten by her father and tied up, Falling Snow sold to the highest bidder, and misery, misery, misery, and here was Jazz, laughing at me and looking happier than I'd ever seen her. What was going on?

"At first, my dad was furious, and he ranted and raved when he found me at the icehouse," Jazz began. "We had a huge fight, and I said I would run away again and again. I told him I would never forgive him if he sold Falling Snow and that I hated him."

"I bet that went down well," mumbled Drummer. I thought so, too. How brave was Jazz?

"But then something extraordinary happened."

"What?" I asked, agog.

"He got upset." Jazz's voice was incredulous. "He told me I meant the world to him, that I was family, close family, and that he thought he had lost me forever."

"Oh!" I said. I'd never pictured Jazz's father as anything but a villain. This was a surprise.

"My dad told me my running away showed him I've inherited my mother's spirit and that he admired me for it. He said he hadn't realized how far I would go to keep Falling Snow. He said he misses my mother so very much, and that was why he had been so distant from me. I remind him of her, you see," she explained.

"Your dad has been terrorizing everyone around here, trying to find you," I told her. "Everyone thinks he's nuts."

"No, he's just my father. He gets angry. He reacts. It's his way. And, of course, I cursed him—but I have removed that curse now. I caused him a lot of worry. We had a long talk, and we both cried, and things are good now between us. It seems we both held in our feelings, and neither of us was willing to talk. We just got angry with each other. That has changed now. We are family again. We are together."

"Are you sure?" I asked, amazed.

"Yes," said Jazz. "When my mom died, I was for Falling Snow and she was for me. My father was for racing, and racing was for him. We should have been for each other. We turned our backs on each other when we should have been united. Our strength is together. It is good now. It is how it should be."

"What about the dog?" said Drummer, like he'd got stuck. I took a deep breath. "What about your dog?" I asked.

"Finally!" exclaimed Drum. "Thank you!"

Jazz's face clouded. "My dad has promised not to sell Falling Snow," she said, "and I've promised not to run away. But I have to prove myself. For a while I can ride out Falling Snow or I can walk out with Kasali, but I can't take them both out at the same time. Just for a while. It is fair. My dad knows I won't go without both of them."

"So Falling Snow is safe?" I said.

Jazz beamed at me and patted her pony's flecked neck. "Yes, she is safe. No more racing. No more talk of her being sold. My dad has agreed. Falling Snow is mine. Really mine. My dad has promised."

"That's so wonderful!" I said. My heart felt lighter, and I took a deep breath. Jazz's disappearance had obviously brought home to her father how much she meant to him. Suddenly, the vision I had of a huge man with scary eyes softened to a friendlier image.

"I'm glad to see you," continued Jazz. "I was riding out to find you—and to thank you. You—and Bean—are good friends. I shall never forget you both."

"Oh, well, you're welcome," I said, suddenly embarrassed.

"It was a good hiding place, the icehouse," Jazz said. "My dad would never have found me if he hadn't been told where to look."

So Jazz knew she had been betrayed! I gulped. Did she know by whom?

"Some people cannot understand how others feel," she said solemnly. "You do. You felt my pain about Falling Snow, and you were brave enough to help me. You are more than a good friend. You are empathic, one who can put herself in another's place. Not everyone can do that. Some people need to be taught how that feels. It can be a hard lesson to learn."

"Er, well…" I mumbled, not knowing how to respond.

"See you, Drummer," said Falling Snow. "Thanks for lending me your exercise sheet."

"No probs. You take care now," Drummer replied.

"Thank you, Pia," Jazz said, with feeling. "I am glad I have been given a chance to help you." She smiled as she turned Falling Snow and rode away through the trees.

I hadn't really understood half of what Jazz had been saying—about me being empathic—or what she had meant about helping me. To be honest, I felt a bit foolish. I'd imagined Jazz beaten and tied up like Kasali—talk about an overactive imagination. Her father had been beside himself with worry, so no wonder he'd acted like a lunatic! With a jolt, I realized that I'd been just as prejudiced about Jazz's father as everyone else had been about the travelers in general.

Staring at the trees through which Jazz and Falling Snow had disappeared, I realized that our vacation was almost over and riding out would soon be confined to the weekends. I probably wouldn't get the opportunity to speak to Jazz again much. I felt quite sad. On the upside, I could enjoy the remainder of my vacation without lugging provisions to the icehouse, without worrying about falling out with everyone else at the yard, without being the outsider. Finally!

I sighed. Thank goodness! My escapade with the travelers was over. I could even forget my dilemma about Jazz being betrayed as it had all turned out all right in the end. Everything was back to normal, and I didn't want to waste any time. I had things to do!

When I got back to the yard, I asked Sophie whether she would be kind enough to give Drummer a blanket clip. She had done a great job with Bluey and Tiffany.

"Of course!" Dee's mom replied, looking at her watch. "I can do it now, if you like, if he doesn't act up."

"Really?" I asked, thrilled. "He'll be as good as gold," I assured her. "Drum's used to being clipped and stands like a statue. Only I don't have any money on me. Can I pay you tomorrow?"

"Of course you can, Pia," she replied. "That's fine."

So I tied Drum outside his stable with a hay net and watched Sophie give him a blanket clip, running the clippers over his neck, his belly, and then, finally, his head. When she'd finished, Sophie stood back and admired her work.

"Mmmm," she said, coiling up the cord to the clippers. "He's a good color. Some bays go a sort of muddy gray underneath their coats, but your Drummer's a lovely red color. Very nice!"

"I heard that!" cried Drum indignantly. "Of course I'm good-looking!"

He was, too. His unclipped back was his usual winter coat, all fiery red and fluffy. His head, neck, and belly were all a deep reddish brown, running into fluffy red legs that tapered into black. With his black mane and tail, I had a three-tone pony, instead of the usual two-tones.

"You look gorgeous!" I told him.

"Yeah, I know, I'm perfection made equine," Drummer replied, modesty not being his strong point.

"I need to do your mane now. It's letting you down."

Drummer rolled his eyes. "Oh, go ahead!"

I lightly trimmed his mane, wrapping the longest hairs from underneath around a mane comb and tugging them out with one quick jerk. It not only shortens the mane, but thins it, too. By the time I'd finished, fistfuls of black mane had joined the short red hair on the ground.

I rugged Drummer up in his green stable rug and gave him a hug.

"There, you'll be able to go twice as fast now!" I whispered to him.

"And buck twice as high," he threatened back.

"Don't you dare!" I told him, grabbing the broom and sweeping up all his surplus hair and throwing it on the trash heap.

As darkness fell, the yard became busy with everyone

filling water buckets and hay nets, mixing feeds, and grooming their ponies. Mrs. Bradley and Henry went for a ride in the school—eventually. Henry must have made a dive for every blade of grass on the way. Leanne's boyfriend, Stuart, of dressage persuasion, arrived to see her, and they both disappeared into Mr. Higgins's stall, giggling. James stayed just long enough to pull Moth in from the field, change her rugs, give me a wave, and fly off again with his mom, and Bean made a big fuss of Drummer and admired his clip.

"Who would have thought it?" she said when I told her about Jazz. "Her dad obviously didn't realize how much he loved Jazz until he lost her. No wonder he was nuts."

"Quite," I said. "I can almost forgive him for behaving so bonkers—although it's easy for me, as I wasn't the one chased or terrorized."

"Drum looks very classy," continued Bean, leaning on Drummer's half door. "He was just a ball of fluff in his winter coat. The clip shows off his head. He looks all noble."

Drum swung an ear in her direction, and I could tell he was pleased.

"I'm going now," I told him, nudging the kick bolt at the bottom of his door over with my toe. "See you tomorrow."

"OK. See ya," Drummer mumbled.

"Are you warm enough in that rug?" I asked him.

"Toasty."

"Are you sure?"

"Are you still here?"

"Oh, OK, I'm going. See you tomorrow."

"Well, I'm not going anywhere, am I?" Drummer replied as I pedaled off.

Jerry was sitting on the sofa when I got in, waiting for Mom to come down. He was wearing his usual outfit of a dazzling, slightly too tight white T-shirt, displaying the result of his many workouts and a pair of tight jeans. It was his night off, and he and Mom were going out. It suddenly hit me that Jerry was Mom's equivalent of Skinny Lynny.

"Still playing with the horsies?" he said, grinning. He thinks it's funny. It so isn't.

I gave him one of my best "I'll indulge you" smiles and nodded. Fortunately, Mom came flying down the stairs at that point. *Unfortunately*, she hadn't heard me come in:

"I'm ready for my sexy personal trainer, and I can't wait to…oh, er, hello, Pia," she said, looking sheepish as she saw me. *Not a moment too soon*, I thought.

They left me in peace, and I raided the freezer, discovering a long lost pizza at the back. What a find! Never had a freezer-burned, squashed, and forgotten pizza tasted so good!

My thoughts returned to Jazz. If she was on such good terms with her father now, maybe, just maybe, Jazz would be able to persuade him not to be so hard on the horses when they raced. Or even stop it altogether. I doubted it, but anything was possible.

I was looking forward to tomorrow. I was going on a long ride with Katy and Bean. With Drum now clipped, he wouldn't sweat, and he'd be up for a good gallop when we got there. I couldn't wait. It was about time we had some fun! I started planning the next few days in earnest. I had to book Drum in for a set of shoes, and I wanted to go to the tack shop in the next town and buy one of those gorgeous jeweled brow bands for Drum, even though I knew he'd hate it. Plus, it was Halloween soon, and James had mentioned a spooky ride around the woods in the dark before we went back to school. That promised to be spooky. I couldn't wait to get back to normality!

But when I got to the yard the next morning, everything was far from normal. A police car was parked outside Mrs. Collins's front door, a policewoman and a policeman were talking to Catriona—a Catriona who was in floods of tears—and everyone was standing around looking shocked and pale.

"Oh, Pia." Katy gasped, running across to me as I leaned my bike against the wall. "You'll never guess what's happened."

"What? What's going on?" I asked, utterly bewildered.

"It's Bambi," cried Katy, with a gulp. "She's been stolen!"

CHAPTER 18

I FELT MY JAW DROP open, and instinctively, I looked across to Drummer's stable. There he was, his head over the door, ears pricked and looking agitated, gazing at the chaos before him.

"No one can understand how—she's stabled virtually in front of Mrs. Collins's front door," continued Katy, close to tears. "And how come the thief only took Bambi? Sophie's totally upset thinking her valuable Lester and Dolly—not to mention the palace on wheels she calls a horse trailer—could be next. And what if the thief comes back and takes Bluey and Drummer and Tiff—and Moth? I mean, it's just so awful! I've texted Bean and James. They'll be here soon."

"Has Cat contacted her freeze branding company, told them Bambi's gone?"

"Of course. They're on it. But she's beside herself, poor Cat. I mean, I can totally understand how she feels. She keeps saying the travelers have taken Bambi. I bet they have, too!"

"I'll ask Drummer who it was," I said. "He'll know whether the travelers did it." I felt indignant on Jazz's behalf. Everyone was bound to jump to conclusions about the travelers, and I was sure Drummer would set the record straight.

Only he didn't. Drummer confirmed that Jazz had been the one who had taken Cat's skewbald mare.

I felt sick. I'd trusted Jazz, helped her, risked my friendships for her. How could she possibly have stolen Bambi after all I'd done for her? I felt totally betrayed—all that garbage she'd spoken about helping me. I couldn't understand it. "Are you sure?" I asked, knowing it was hopeless. Drummer wouldn't lie.

I got the answer I deserved. "Of course I'm sure! She led her along the grass verge by the path so her hooves wouldn't make a noise on the gravel. I neighed and whinnied, but that crazy old lady with the slipper fetish must have been sound asleep because she didn't stir. And that useless dog of hers ignored me, too."

Squish wasn't much of a guard dog, I had to agree.

"We have to find her!" Drum said. "We just *have* to!" Poor Drum. He so loved Bambi. At that moment, Bean arrived, throwing first her bike onto the gravel, then herself at Tiffany's half door. The palomino mare freaked and practically sat down in shock.

"Thank goodness you're still here!" she said dramatically. Then she turned to Catriona. "Oh, Cat, I'm so sorry. I'm sure the police will find Bambi."

Catriona was in no mood for sympathy. "It's all your fault!" she yelled. "You and Mia had to get friendly with the traveler girl, didn't you? Only it's my pony that gets stolen, not hers!"

Bean took a step backward, shocked. "But—but—" she stammered.

"What are you talking about?" asked Katy.

"So don't pretend you care now, Charlotte Beanie,"

continued Cat, "because I don't believe you. I told all of you that this would happen, but you didn't listen."

"Oh, Cat, I know Jazz wouldn't have taken Bambi. Honest, she wouldn't," said Bean.

"Have you been friendly with Jazz?" Katy asked.

"Now, now, let's all calm down, shall we?" said the policeman. "Who's Jazz?"

"Actually," I said, "I think Jazz did steal Bambi."

Catriona turned her tearstained face toward me and practically screamed that it was all my fault and that I was that witch Jazz's friend and that I'd helped her run away.

"It should be your pony that's missing!" she shouted. "He was supposed to take Drummer!"

"What?" I cried. "What are you talking about?"

The policewoman interrupted, wanting to know how I knew about Jazz.

Oh, pooh.

Katy got it, and because she was the only one making any sense, the police asked her to explain. Katy told them about my pony whispering title. The policewoman and the policeman exchanged skeptical glances. Katy showed them the newspaper clipping (it was still stuck on the notice board in the tack room, which Cat pretended to ignore every time she went in there) that had announced me to the world. The policeman lifted one eyebrow, and the policewoman sucked in her cheeks in a *now I've heard it all* kind of way.

"So you expect us to believe that your pony"—the

policeman gestured toward Drummer who looked him in the eye and stared him out—"the brown one over there, is our only witness."

"And according to him," the policewoman continued, "one of the traveler kids took off with the missing pony."

"Why are you all talking to Pia?" screamed Cat, thoroughly losing it. "It isn't about her for once, it isn't about her stupid, dumb, lying, pony whispering crap. It's about *my* pony. Why are you all still here asking questions? Why aren't you raiding the travelers' camp and getting Bambi back? They've taken *the wrong pony*. All this talk, talk, talk. DO SOMETHING for goodness sake!"

"What do you mean," I said, "'the wrong pony'?"

"Cat's right," said Katy to the police. "You're just wasting time."

"We'll be the judge of that, young lady," growled the policeman.

I looked at Catriona. "Cat, I didn't mean for this to happen…" I trailed off helplessly. Cat just dropped her head into her hands and howled.

I feel awful, but it is nothing to how Cat must be feeling, I thought. How could Jazz do such a terrible, terrible thing? She of all people ought to know how Cat would feel. Jazz had run away to keep Falling Snow. Didn't she realize that Cat felt the same way about Bambi? Even given the circumstances, it was unforgivable.

After a discussion, the police decided to report back to the police station, and Cat went with them.

"Well, I'm not staying here!" snorted Katy, running toward the tack room for Bluey's saddle and bridle.

"Where are you going?" I shouted, even though I already knew.

"To the Sloping Field!" Katy replied. "I don't know what you two have been up to, but we have to see whether Bambi's with the travelers."

"At last!" yelled Drummer.

"Wait for me!" shouted Bean.

I fled to the tack room for Drummer's tack, and in just a few moments, Katy, Bean, and I were all mounted in the yard. Drummer had straw in his mane and tail, and Tiffany sported a huge stable stain down her hind, but there was no time to worry about standards. Bigger things were at stake.

Then James arrived.

"We're going to the travelers' camp," explained Katy, reining in Bluey by the tack room as James ran for Moth's tack. "Jazz has taken Bambi, and we're going to get her back."

This is news, I thought. *How exactly are we going to do that?*

Breaking the world speed record for tacking up, James jammed his helmet on his head and vaulted into Moth's saddle as the chestnut half reared, half cantered up the drive behind us. Drummer felt sturdy and determined under me. He was going to rescue his beloved Bambi.

We raced into the woods and along the bridle path. Tiffany, sensing that this was a serious mission, for once didn't shy at every little thing. I could hear Bluey being all indignant at Bambi's abduction, could hear Drummer vowing to rescue his skewbald heroine, and could make out Tiffany saying she was sorry she'd ever been nice to Falling Snow if her human was such a nasty piece of work. And as we urged on the ponies, my head churned with thoughts, about Jazz and loyalty, and wasted words and friendship, of betrayal and revenge. The wrong pony, Cat had said. What had she meant?

At last we approached the Sloping Field and, in the shade of the trees, pulled up and calmed down.

"What's the plan?" whispered Bean.

"We'd better not confront Jazz," said Katy. "After all, the travelers could get violent."

"Well, if Bambi's there, we'll just ride in and take her!" said James.

"No, James, we need the police to deal with it. We'll call them and tell them she's here," Katy replied.

That sounded good to me.

We crept forward and came out in a line at the top of the hill, looking down at the Sloping Field, expecting to see Bambi.

Instead, we saw an empty field with bare, grazed rings of grass where horses had been tethered, trash that had been left behind, a van with no wheels, dumped and forgotten.

The travelers had gone. And they'd taken Bambi with them.

CHAPTER 19

No one spoke. Then I heard Drummer groan. His darling Bambi had been taken, goodness-knows-where.

"Oh, no, poor Bambi," whispered Bean.

"They couldn't have gone far," James said.

"I don't understand why they'd steal only one pony," said Katy, shaking her head. "Why steal just Bambi? What's the point when all our ponies were there?"

"And Bambi's so distinctively marked," I added. "They can't hope to get away with it."

"Not to mention her freeze brand," Katy pointed out. "I just don't get it."

I did. Suddenly, I got it big-time. Suddenly, everything Cat had said at the yard became dazzlingly clear. I got it, all right.

"I don't think Jazz ever intended to take Bambi *with her*," I said, my mind working overtime.

"What?" said Drummer, his ears swiveling around to hear me.

"No, I think she took Bambi to teach Cat a lesson." Bean, Katy, and James all turned to look at me. "She wanted Cat to understand how she felt about Falling Snow…" I explained. "And what it was like to lose a pony. A pony you love! I don't think Bambi's with Jazz at all."

"Now you're talking nonsense," said Bean. "First Bambi's with Jazz, then she isn't. Then she took her, then she didn't. Make up your mind."

"Are you saying," said James, "that Jazz took Bambi, but she doesn't have her now? And Jazz did it to get Cat back for telling her father where she was hiding?"

"What?" shouted Bean.

"Oh, yes, Cat told Jazz's father about the icehouse," James said, like it was all so simple.

"Don't just hit and run like that James," said Katy, exasperated. "Explain!"

"It was something Cat said after Jazz's father yelled at us that day out riding," explained James. "She said if she knew where Jazz was hiding, she'd tell him. Then she said Bean knew something."

"No way!" exclaimed Bean, all defensive.

"Well, that's what I said," added James.

"She was right," I said miserably. The game was up.

"What?" said Katy. "Both of you?"

"You're a dark horse, Bean," said James, "but not dark enough. Cat must have followed you and discovered where you and Pia were hiding Jazz."

Suddenly, I breathed in sharply as I realized something else. Cat had traded the knowledge of Jazz's hiding place to her father for his promise to take Drummer. That was what Cat had meant—Drummer was supposed to be the missing pony. What a horrible, horrible thing to do. How could she? When Jazz had said she was going to help me, she must have persuaded her father not to do it. Jazz hadn't betrayed me at all—at least, not if we could find where she'd hidden Bambi.

"Cat must have told Jazz's dad and got him to promise to steal Drummer," I said.

"Drummer?" asked James.

"I think that was Cat's plan. To teach me a lesson, to hit back because—" I stopped, suddenly aware my thoughts had hijacked my mouth. I couldn't say out loud that Cat was upset about not going out with James anymore. I couldn't be that mean.

"OK, OK, but where is Bambi, if you're right?" Katy asked, cutting to the chase, as always.

"Shhhh!" said Drummer, his head up, his ears twitching.

"What is it?" I asked, stroking his clipped neck.

"I hear something."

"What's going on?" asked Katy.

"It's Drum," I explained. "He says he can hear something."

Everyone held their breath—which wasn't very helpful as the wind whistled through the trees, changing direction, hindering, helping.

"It's Bambi!" exclaimed Drum, snorting.

"I can hear her neighing!" I told the others.

"So let's go!" shouted Bean. It wasn't that simple. The other ponies pricked their ears, and an equine argument broke out.

"It's coming from over there…"

"Where?"

"Over there!"

"No, no, this way."

"Are you sure?"

"Positive! Oh, no wait a minute…"

"Is it me, or can anyone else hear what sounds like lions roaring?"

"Not now, Tiff!"

"I thought it was from that direction. But now I'm not so sure."

"Definitely this way, come on!"

Drummer turned and set off purposefully, the other ponies following, their riders sitting quietly. Everyone was silent now, enabling the ponies to hear any sounds Bambi might be throwing out for us to hear.

We rode down to the lake. Then up, up the hill. Then we stopped.

"Oh, I can hear her!" exclaimed Katy, and we cantered on in through the trees, bursting through holly trees and rhododendrons to a hidden clearing and the icehouse—of course!

And there, in her stable rug, tied to a tree with a length of rope was Bambi, neighing with relief that she'd been found.

"Thank goodness!" she cried, as we all came to a halt. James leaped out of the saddle, throwing Moth's reins to Bean so he could untie Cat's skewbald mare from the tree.

"I've been here half the night, all alone!"

"Oh, how awful," sympathized Tiffany. "You must have been terrified. Are you all right? Have you seen any lions?"

"Yes, yes, fine, thanks. A bit shaky, that's all. And I'm thirsty. What do you mean, *lions?*"

"We'll get you home soon," said Bluey.

"What kept you?" said Bambi, rubbing her nose on James's sleeve. James stroked her wide, white blaze. "I've been neighing for ages!"

"Drummer heard you," Tiffany told her. "It's all thanks to him we're here."

Drummer said nothing. He just gazed at Bambi, lost for words. Bambi gazed back, and I held my breath. Would she be her usual, grumpy, frowning self?

Bambi took a step toward Drummer. She pricked her ears forward and shyly leaned forward, gently nuzzling Drum's bay nose.

"Thanks, Drummer," she whispered.

I felt quite choked up. My pony was a hero. But then, I knew that.

Katy broke the spell.

"What's that on Bambi's rug?" she asked, pointing.

We all turned to look. Something had been chalked onto Bambi's rug. Scrawled across the shoulder was some writing.

"Six words," James said, grimly.

"What do they say?" asked Bean. I knew what they were going to be. I didn't have to see the writing.

"*'Now you know what it's like',*" read James.

Chapter 20

"THIS IS *SOOOO* DIFFICULT!" exclaimed Bean, grasping Tiffany's white mane.

"At least Tiffany's got a backbone to help you stay on," I said, trotting past her on Drum. "Drummer's so round, it's like sitting on a barrel."

"How rude! Barrel my behind!" Drum retorted. "Just for that, I'm going to wobble about a bit…"

"No! Don't!" I pleaded, clutching his mane as Drum did a sort of shimmy along the short side of the outdoor school. It was like riding on jelly. I was glad it was getting dark because I knew I looked anything but proficient.

"How come it was so easy for Jazz?" Katy asked, making it look just as easy on Bluey, who was shuffling around, barely lifting his knees to make it more comfortable for his beloved Katy to sit while he trotted. I was sure Drummer was lifting his knees higher on purpose.

We'd taken off our saddles and lined them up on the fence. It had seemed like a great idea to try riding bareback like Jazz, but I for one was finding it terribly difficult to stay central on Drum's slippery back. My admiration for Jazz soared—like it wasn't high enough already.

"Have either of you heard of an ice tail?" asked Bean, bringing Tiffany to a halt in the corner. I steered Drum alongside her.

"I have. But I can't remember what it is."

"Bean," began Katy, doing a circle next to us, "why are you asking all these questions? Are you doing some kind of home study course or something?"

Bean looked a bit sheepish, twiddling Tiffany's long mane around her fingers self-consciously.

"Come on, Bean, out with it!" I demanded.

"Well, if you must know, I'm entering a competition in *PONY* Magazine."

"What's the prize?" I asked.

"A riding vacation."

"No one ever wins those things," said Katy, her eyebrows almost meeting together on her forehead as she concentrated on keeping her weight central over Bluey's back. Bluey put his head down and sneezed, pulling her forward and spoiling it.

"They do so, Katy!" protested Bean. "One girl wrote in about the awesome vacation she won last year."

"Well, you probably won't," Katy replied.

"I won't if I don't enter, that's for sure."

"Exmoor ponies!" I yelled, making Drummer jump. He gave a meaningful sigh. I don't think he was very impressed with the bareback idea.

"Is that a new swear word?" giggled Bean.

"No, Exmoor ponies have ice tails. They grow an extra bit of hair at the very top, so that rain and snow and stuff just slide off, and that's what it's called. It was a question in a quiz night I went to once at my old yard."

"Thanks for helping me, Pia, you're a good friend," Bean said. "Not like some people..." she added, giving Katy a dirty look. Katy didn't care.

"I'm going to try a jump!" she yelled, turning Bluey toward a small jump at the other end of the school. Bluey broke into a smooth canter and popped over, with Katy making a good show of it. She cantered back with a huge grin on her face.

"You try!" she cried, patting Bluey's neck.

"I don't think so," mumbled Bean. I didn't blame her—Tiffany has the oddest jumping style I've ever seen. "I might try a canter, though. Come on, Tiff." Tiffany broke into a slow canter with Bean getting more confident as she turned a corner.

"Look, I can do it without holding on to her mane..." Bean began, holding up her hands.

"WHAT'S THAT ON THE FENCE???" exclaimed Tiffany, shying at the saddles and doing a one-eighty in about a millisecond. Without her saddle, Bean didn't stand a chance of staying on. Instead, she flew over Tiffany's golden shoulder to land on the ground with a splat. Katy and I held our breath.

"Oww, that is so not funny," grumbled Bean, picking herself up off the ground and dusting herself off, clearly not hurt.

"Cool dismount!" Katy laughed.

"Look, Mom, no hands is so not your style." I giggled.

"Oh, thanks for your sympathy!" Bean complained,

retrieving Tiffany from where she'd wedged herself between Drum and Bluey.

"Honestly, Tiff," said Drummer. "You are an idiot. Those saddles have been there forever."

"Well, they looked different when I approached them in canter," Tiffany explained, sniffing. "It must be the light."

"You've got a nice dung stain on your fleece," Katy pointed out to Bean.

"Oh, well, I'll just turn it inside out, then no one will be any the wiser," Bean replied airily.

"Do it before you get back on, else Tiff will dump you again," I suggested.

"I wasn't dumped!" retorted Bean huffily. "I merely dismounted without permission."

Collecting our saddles, we took the ponies back to the yard in time to see Dolly clattering up the ramp of Sophie's luxury horse trailer.

"Horse of the Year Show, here we come! Wish me luck!" Dolly shouted as Sophie tied her up and checked her tail guard.

"Good luck!" chorused all the ponies.

"Don't come back without a ribbon!" shouted Bluey.

"Are you ready, Dee?" Sophie yelled, fastening the ramp and climbing into the cab.

Dee flew out of the tack room, making Tiffany flinch. "Coming! See you guys—wish me luck!"

"Good luck!" we all chorused, echoing the ponies.

"Do you think she'll win?" asked Bean.

"No," Katy replied. "But she says she'll be happy if they make the final lineup. Just qualifying is huge, apparently."

"Funny time to be going to a show," mused Drummer.

"They're staying overnight so they'll be all fresh in the morning," I explained.

We all waved as the horse trailer rolled along the gravel, catching on overhanging branches along the drive on its way to the road.

I rugged up Drummer and kissed him on the nose. He hates me doing that, but I can't resist it—he's got such a cute, soft, black nose just begging to be kissed! I could hear Bambi next door, back home again after her ordeal. Cat had been overjoyed that we'd found her—although the fact that my ability to hear the ponies had enabled us to discover Bambi wasn't appreciated. It was all very complicated, but I was past caring. I mean, Cat had planned for Jazz's dad to steal Drummer! I'd never forgive her for that—I don't care how upset she might have been about James. It was a totally mean thing to do.

I collected my bike and stood by the tack room, watching Drummer in the gathering darkness. He stuck his head out over his top door and snorted. Next door, I could make out Bambi's two-tone head appearing over her half door. Usually she pulled faces at Drummer, but this evening she looked across at him and snorted softly back.

Drummer had been the one who had rescued Bambi. Could it be possible that while Cat and I were even more at war than ever, it had brought Drum and Bambi together?

"It's great to have you home, Bambi," I heard Drummer say.

"Don't think you've got a chance!" I heard Bambi reply. Only her voice was softer than her usual rebuff. It seemed Drummer had a long way to go before Bambi let down all her defenses—but it was a start!

We said our good nights, and I cycled home. It had been a very peculiar vacation, what with one thing and another. But still, I reflected as I let myself into the house, it had been anything but dull!

"Hi, Mom!" I shouted.

"Oh, hi, hon," my mom replied.

Something wasn't right. She wasn't wearing her gym gear, the TV was on, and she had a glass of wine in her hand.

"Not going to the gym?" I asked her.

"No. I'm a bit tired."

"Oh?" I waited.

She screwed up her face and gave me a crooked grin. "I'm a bit tired of Jerry, too."

What did I tell you? Cue the novelty wearing off. I feigned surprise.

"Yeah." Mom sighed. "He's a little egotistic—always admiring himself in the mirror. Well, any highly polished surface really—shop windows, computer monitors. I caught him checking himself out in his knife the other evening."

"He's got a knife!!!" I cried, my imagination catapulting into overdrive.

Mom laughed. "Knife and *fork*—we were in a restaurant!" she explained.

We sat in silence for a moment. So Jerry had got the boot, eh?

"Do you know what, Pia? I'm pretty hungry, and I don't think a salad is going to cut it."

Now that was music to my ears. I held my breath. What was it going to be? Pizza? Burger? Pasta? All good. All better than a salad.

Mom got up and went into the kitchen, and I heard her rummaging around in the cupboards.

"How does ham and eggs sound?"

"Great!" I replied.

"I know I've got a tin of ham in here somewhere…" I heard her mumble.

Ahhhh! Flashback! The just-in-case canned ham! My mom could look in the cupboard until the cows came home, but there was no canned ham in there. It was still at the icehouse. How could I turn this around?

"Mom."

"Yes, honey?"

"I tell you what I really, *really* want."

"Go on."

"Indian food!"

It all went quiet. I held my breath.

"Great idea. Get your coat!"

Phew. Sometimes, as Bean says, a girl has to think on her feet!